Growing Up and Other Disasters

Book One of the Crantz Chronicles

Mandi Hayes-Spencer

Cover Photo Copyright © 2012 Divine Revelation Photography

Cover Model Chelsea West

Cover design by Gretchen Flint, Quirk House Books.

Book design and production by Quirk House Books

Editing by "Triple J." Rekulak Senior Editor, Quirk House Books

Author photograph by Divine Revelation Photography

ISBN 978-0615647982

DEDICATION

This book is for my dad who told me that I had the ability to one day write a book that would change the world, my mom who gave me the courage to go out and do it, my husband who loves me flaws and all and my son, who is truly my life's greatest work. I love you Dad, Mom, Hub and Gavin.

CONTENTS

ACKNOWLEDGMENTS

When I started writing this book, my dad was busy fighting an uphill battle with Alzheimer's disease. I was about halfway through when he lost that fight and we lost him forever. If I hadn't had the constant support of my family, my friends, my editor and even my dog Stella, I might not ever have finished. I would like to thank them all from the bottom of my heart. So to my Mom, Hub, Gavin, Eddie, Melissa, Colin, Allyson, Katie, Steven, Triple-J the Super Editor, The Bond Family and The Greenup County Beacon, Molly, Junior, Becky and The Spencer Family, The Myers, The Conley Seven, Amy V., Dr. and Dr. Qualls, my Facebook Homies and the list goes on...I love you all more than you will ever know.

"IT'S NOT THE FALL THAT KILLS YOU; IT'S THE SUDDEN STOP AT THE END."

-DOUGLAS ADAMS
THE HITCHHIKER'S GUIDE TO THE GALAXY

1 WHERE IN THE HELL IS MILLIE CRANTZ?

All I ever wanted out of life was a little slice of normal. Instead, I got a butt load of crazy with a side of Holy crap.

I suppose that's why I am standing in the middle of a cemetery in the rain, wondering how I got here.

As I look around, I see a lot of familiar faces and some not so familiar. The only similarity between them all is the grief that shows in their expressions.

We are all gathered in a circle around the grave, some of us behind others where we can squeeze in well enough to see. The casket is propped up above the hole in which it will soon be buried. Surrounding it is the green turf you see at most funerals, used to cover up the pile of dirt left over when the grave was made and a welcome camouflage to the funeral party. Nobody wants to see the actual dirt that will cover their loved ones once the service is over.

The coffin itself is beautiful. Well, for a coffin,

anyways. The dark brown mahogany is shiny and silver handles embellished with intricate curly cues run its length making it look strangely sophisticated. The spray of carefully arranged wild flowers that have been laid over the top vary in color, their vines reaching over the sides as if it is their duty to protect the person inside.

The rain starts coming down harder and I realize I am the only one without an umbrella. I do my best to scoot over and share the umbrella of my neighbor, an older lady wearing the world's biggest hat, but she inches away from me and pretends not to notice I am being pelted by ginormic raindrops.

How rude.

I should have dressed more weather appropriate. But I was, as usual, running late and in a hurry to get here. I am regretting my rush when my black patent leather heels start to fill up with cold rain water and my feet go from an uncomfortable tingle to completely numb.

After five or so minutes, my long, wildly curly dark hair plasters itself to my head. The part of my legs sticking out from my black, knee length pencil skirt are turning an unattractive shade of blue and the only warm piece of clothing I am wearing, a red wool sweater, is making me so itchy I can't do anything but squirm around in discomfort.

This sucks.

My heels have long since sunk into the rain soaked ground. I am completely stuck to the spot where I am standing and the more it rains, the deeper they sink.

Doing my best to unstick myself, I slowly yank

my left foot up. My foot comes quickly out of my shoe, but the shoe stays put. I stumble, almost knocking over the lady with the hat.

Powerless to stop the impulse, a very loud, "*Dammit!*" rolled out of my mouth.

I froze where I stood-one shoe on, another stuck in the mud, praying nobody heard me.

Luckily, nobody seems to notice. After some thought, I decide the mess it would cause to free myself isn't worth the embarrassment and just stand there lopsided like an idiot.

I look up from my feet and, through the sheets of rain, see that someone is staring at me. Great. I thought nobody had noticed my outburst but apparently somebody did.

The first thing I see is her eyes. They're the brightest blue I have ever seen and just looking at her makes you feel like she knows everything about you.

She is sitting in a row with the rest of the deceased's family members. She is wearing a simple black dress with a grey sweater to keep her warm along with a little black hat that allows just a small tuft of her graying hair to peek out from underneath. Her face is aged and I am guessing she is at least in her 80's, if not older.

As we look at each other, her sorrow is almost tangible. Like if I reached out to touch it, that icy cold grief would travel up my finger, through my arm and make its way straight to my heart. I shiver, but not from the cold of the weather.

Then, without warning, her face shifts and a smile appears. At first I think she's laughing at me because I'm standing here in only one shoe looking like a slightly deranged wet dog. But, no, something tells me that her smile means so much more than that.

I can't bear to look at her anymore, so I look back down to my feet and stand stock still until the pastor is finished with the service.

As the slosh of departing footsteps sound around me, I stay put. I don't want anybody to see me digging my shoes out of the mud. I'll just wait until everyone leaves and make an ass out of myself in private. I pretend to be praying, looking down at the ground so nobody tries to talk to me and I can get out of here as quickly as possible.

The last car door slams and I lift my head, only to find that I am nose to nose with the little old lady that was staring at me.

"It's good to see you." She says, lifting her hand to touch my cheek. Her hands are soft with age and strangely familiar.

"Good to see you, too." I reply, not having a clue who she is but doing my best to pretend like I do.

"Quit the crap, Millie. You don't recognize me, do you?"

A little shocked by her terse reply, I consider saying, 'Of course I do!" But, those eyes of hers tell me she won't buy it.

"Sorry, I don't. You look familiar but I'm not sure who you are."

"That figures" she says, pursing her lips in thought before smiling and letting out a chuckle. "You never were the brightest crayon in the box."

"Well, that was uncalled for. Who the heck are you, anyways? Well, besides from some rude old lady in a cemetery?"

"It doesn't matter. What matters is, I know you. I know you really well and in time, you will remember me. For now, I want you to take these."

She digs down in her huge black purse and feels around for a minute before she says, "Ah ha!" She pulls out a pair of navy blue tennis shoes with lime green shoestrings and holds them out for me.

I gasped. I may not know this lady, but I know those shoes.

They're my shoes, the shoes that were a present from my friend Maggie on my sixteenth birthday. They're the shoes that I wore every day after that until they were so ragged I couldn't wear them anymore.

I start to speak, but it only comes out as a series of stutters. It sounded a little bit like I was trying to speak Chinese.

"Will you hush? You sound ridiculous. I will explain if you just take these." She stretched her arm out and dangled the shoes in front of my face. "I'm an old lady and this cold is doing a number on my arthritis."

I gently took the shoes away from her and examine them. They look almost brand new.

"I've got to go now. Good luck, Millie."

I look up from the shoes and realize that she's walking away. What the heck? That wasn't an explanation.

"Hey! You said you would explain!" I started to run forward to catch her, forgetting I was still staked in the mud by one of my heels. I do my best to catch my balance, but end up doing a not-so-graceful face plant in the mud, anyways.

"Ah, hell! Why is this crap always happening to

me?" I yelled in frustration.

I got up, wiped the dirt from my eyes and started to scream curse words at her when I realized she was gone. It was like she'd wiggled her nose Samantha from Bewitched style and poofed herself out of here.

What the heck?

Making things even better, I'd lost both of my heels and am officially barefoot. The tennis shoes are still sitting in the rain where I dropped them, filling up with water but relatively clean despite the fall.

Without a better option, I dump them out, slide my feet in with a squish and let out a squeak as my feet register the cold.

And then, for reasons I can't quite explain, I find myself walking over to the still exposed mahogany casket. For a long time, I just stared at it, unable to think of anything else but my strange exchange with the little old lady just moments before and the feelings in my gut that tell me the person in front of me is important.

Who was that lady? I feel like I should know, but I can't quite get a grip on my thoughts. It's like they've become as slippery as the mud. One minute I feel like I have a hold on one, the next minute it's gone.

I look down at my shoes, still confused, but comforted by them. All the miles I walked in them as a kid is part of what brought me here today and I have to wonder if they have some kind of meaning.

It would have been nice if my elderly visitor had given me a few more answers instead of just leaving me here with a bunch of questions.

An umbrella wouldn't hurt much right now, either.

Exhausted, I looked up to the sky, closed my eyes and felt the rain coming down hard on my face. I said a silent little prayer, asking for the strength to get through whatever this is.

My mind was alive with thousands of different questions, but I thought I would send up the most important one of all, just in case the big man upstairs felt like answering it for me.

"Why am I here?"

2 MEET THE CRANTZ FAMILY

Somebody was breathing on my face.

"Time to wake up, stupid. Mom's been yelling for you for about ten minutes now and Grandma Lucille told me to come in here and make sure you hadn't been abducted by aliens. She's been watching Unsolved Mysteries again."

I cracked one eyelid open only a little. I knew who it was. I would recognize that whiny, annoying, pubescent crackle anywhere.

"If you don't get your head out of my face, I swear I will smack you. And, seriously, your breath is going to melt my face off." Opening my eyes the rest of the way only confirmed what I'd already known. My brother George Jr. and his big ugly head had breached my comfort zone.

Instead of leaving me alone, he blew directly in my face. I was up and chasing him out of my room before he knew what hit him. He was so preoccupied with looking behind him to see how close I was, he didn't notice he was headed straight for the doorframe.

With a thump, he ran square into the side of our kitchen doorway. I was laughing at him until my mom ran into the kitchen with a look of panic on her face.

Clearly she'd heard the collision.

My mom barely hits a couple of inches over five feet, has short, curly brown hair and dresses like every other older woman I've ever known. This morning she had on pleated khakis and a blue jean colored button up shirt, tidily stuffed in. All of her clothes were always starched and creased within an inch of their lives. The look on her face said she wasn't happy.

"What in the hell are you all doing? No, no, don't tell me. As long as nobody needs stitches, a neck brace or a tooth capped, it doesn't matter. George, for God's sakes, get out of the floor. Millie, help him up! I don't have time for this today!" She started to turn around to head back the way she came, but turned around, gave me a wink and said, "Oh, and Happy Sweet Sixteen, brat."

I hollered a quick thanks and looked down at the lump of dummy still lying at my feet.

I put my hand down to help him up like I was told, but he smacked it away. In retaliation, I quietly kicked him in the shin and walked back down the hall to my room. In response to my brother's girly whines, I heard my mom mutter something that sounded a lot like, "Why did I have two of them?" before I slammed my door.

"Moment of truth!" I said to the reflection looking back at me from my bedroom mirror. I turned sideways and examined my new sixteen year old form. While the red and green plaid pajama shorts and oversized t-shirt I was wearing weren't very figure flattering, I didn't care. I was more interested in my chest area and whether or not I had, overnight, developed a full grown set of miracle boobs. After practically spinning around in circles, I realized that at no angle did I look any different.

No, they were still the same size. What. A. Crock.

Giving up, I riffled through the pile of clothes lying in the bottom of my closet and found a pair of jeans that I'd recently frayed at the bottom, a t-shirt, a green and blue flannel button up and a ratty old pair of tennis shoes that had seen better days. I carefully styled my hair in a way that made the shoulder length dark curls appear both messy and fixed, slapped on the black eyeliner and mascara that had become my staple and I was ready to go.

I grabbed my book bag and gave myself a once over in the mirror, confirming that I was, indeed, the poster child for 90's cliché's.

Mission accomplished.

My mom takes breakfast seriously. You leave the house without eating breakfast and you are risking life and limb, so not one person in the Crantz house leaves the premises without at least a piece of bacon in our hand. I tossed my book bag onto the floor and plopped down in a chair at the kitchen table to wait.

Wearing her trademark house coat and fuzzy blue, ankle high bedroom slippers, Grandma Lucille shuffled into the kitchen with a yawn. With every step she took, her house shoes made a scuffing sound on the linoleum floor.

Grandma Lucille is my mom's mom. She's a tiny woman with a tightly curled head of grey hair and wrinkles from head to toe. She may look like your average 70-something year old woman, but has the mind of a 20-something with oats to sew and was born without a brain-to-mouth filter. She moved in with us last year when my Papaw Vernon died.

"Good, Lord. The older I get, the worse these mornings are. When ya get wrinkles like me, it takes a good hour just to peel your saggy ol' butt outta bed. "

"Morning, grandma." I said with a smile. Even though she was about half nuts, I loved the woman dearly.

"And, to you, little Millie girl. Happy Birthday! Say, how's about you go down to the bingo hall with me and Mrs. Potter to celebrate your sixteen years? Her husband had a little accident with some of them Viagra pills, so I'm going to get her out of the house for a little while."

"Well, as tempting as that sounds, I just figured I would go over and hang out with Maggie." I looked pointedly at my mom's back as she leaned over the stove to push the bacon around. "Since I decided that I would NOT have a party this year, I'm going to hang out with some friends."

"Well, your loss. Hey, Earnestine, you want to go? That husband of yours is about as fun as a colonoscopy. We could have a girl's night out." As she waited for an answer, she casually popped out her teeth and gave them a glance before putting them back in again. The sight of it made me throw up in my mouth a little bit.

Without so much as turning around to face her, my mom replied, "I'd rather set my hair on fire."

"Suit yourself. I swear I wonder if you weren't switched at birth."

My mom just shook her head and started stacking the bacon on a plate. As soon as the first piece hit the porcelain, my dad was walking through the kitchen door with my brother on his heels. He had a knack for showing up at the breakfast table every morning just as it was time to eat. I suspect he did this to avoid Grandma Lucille.

My dad, George Crantz, works at the local steel plant as Civil Engineer and always wears a white button up shirt, navy blue, black or brown slacks and black wing tip shoes. And no matter how much we tease him about it, he's the last man on earth to still sport a pocket protector.

He's mostly bald, but has a short, salt and pepper ring of hair that makes a perfect horse shoe around his head. And, even though he has a stern look about him, has a pretty good sense of humor. The only exception to that rule is Grandma Lucille. He thinks she's one crayon short of a full box and she thinks he's a horse's ass.

"Good morning." He poured a cup of coffee and came over to my side of the table, giving me a kiss on the top of my head. "Happy sixteenth, Millie May. It's hard to believe you're old enough to drive a car."

I started to remind him about my driving test later, but he held up his hand to stop me. "Yes, I know. I'll pick you up from school around 1:00. Until then, allow me to sit here in peace and drink my coffee without images of you driving a car into the living room flashing through my mind."

"Anyways" Grandma Lucille said with a dismissive wave of her hand, "I was talking to my friend Jeanie at the grocery store the other day and she was telling me about when her granddaughter Winnie turned sixteen. They took her out for a box of them prophylactic devices. She saw a show on television that said kids start having…"

I stood up without pushing my chair back and almost knocked the table over, my mom dropped her bacon, plate and all, and my dad just sat his coffee down and put his head in his hands. I ran out of that house so fast you'd think somebody threw a firecracker in my pants.

And you thought your family was weird?

3 NEW SHOES

I was born and raised in Flatwoods, Kentucky, a small town that sits almost directly on the border of Ohio.

Contrary to popular belief, not all of us Kentuckians are hillbillies who run around sporting mullets and wife beaters. We also try to limit the amount of time we spend being shoeless, pregnant, drunk and loud, but like all the other 49 states in America, we do have folks around here who stay that way.

Overall, we get a bad rap, thanks mostly to movies. We're actually quite nice, believe it or not.

Mess with one of us, however, and we'll not hesitate to push aside that down home charm and give you a good old fashioned Kentucky Fried ass kicking if you need it.

Despite my teenage claims to the contrary, I love Flatwoods. The houses are small, mostly middle class and tidy, the people are friendly and we're one of the few towns left in America where people still feel comfortable enough to leave their doors unlocked and their keys in the ignition without worrying some hooligan will come along and steal them.

Nothing really exciting happens around here, so when I ran outside screaming, "Oh no! NO NO!" it didn't raise any alarms. Our neighbor Mrs. Fallcheck was outside watering her flowers and just kind of looked at me, gave a half wave and went back to the task at hand without so much as batting an eyelash. If we lived in a bigger city, somebody might have called the police or something.

How would I explain that one?

"It wasn't my fault, officer. My grandmother started talking about condoms at the breakfast table and I panicked. "

Right.

My bus stop was situated at the very end of the block from our house and was always jam packed with kids from neighboring houses.

Luckily, my best friend Maggie didn't live too far away from me and both of our stops were in walking distance from where we lived. We took turns every day and made it so that one day I would walk to hers and the next, she would walk to mine. Today was her day to meet me at mine.

Maggie had a car, but her parent's insisted that it was a waste of money in gas to drive to school when the bus would do it for them, so she never got to drive unless it was a special occasion.

As I rounded the corner she was the first person I saw. Actually, you could probably pick Maggie out of a crowd from outer space. She is always wearing a tie dyed shirt that could easily burn your retinas out of your head if you looked at it in the sun too long. Her penchant for wildly colored Doc Marten boots didn't help matters, but it suited her.

She and my friend Chris, who was wearing a shirt that had a picture of a chicken on it with a thought bubble above it that just said, 'Moo', were having what looked to be a very serious conversation until they spotted me. As a unit, they both pivoted towards me and walked in unison, stopping halfway between where I was and where they had started out.

I smiled because, seriously, what a couple of weirdoes.

I started to ask what was going on, but then I realized they were moving like they had purpose. Chris pointed over to a kid who everybody called Klingsley because of his affection for all things Star Trek. After making some kind of hand gesture that I guess was meant to beam him somewhere, he ran over to a small CD player that was sitting in the grass that I hadn't noticed before.

For the next three or so minutes, I was serenaded with what can only be described as a really bad synchronized ballet routine to You Say It's Your Birthday. I was laughing along with everybody else until Chris, in an attempt to hoist Maggie over his head Dirty Dancing style, stepped off the curb and they both went tumbling to the pavement.

Klingsley quickly cut off the music and we all stopped breathing while we waited for somebody to move.

Rolling over onto her back, an annoyed Maggie yelled, "Dammit! You dropped me! That was totally not part of our routine, you amateur! I think I've broken my face! "

I went over to help her up. "That was awesome. I especially liked that last part where you fell on your asses."

Maggie gave me one of her best eye rolls and we both went and leaned over Chris who was still splayed out face up in the middle of the road. He was blinking, so we helped him up while he groaned in protest. "Maggie, I think you permanently damaged something. You're going to have to be the one to explain to my mom why I won't be able to produce any grandchildren."

As Maggie and I were brushing all of the little pieces of road off of him, the bus pulled up and we quickly piled in. Chris was still walking funny and looked like he might be a little constipated, but otherwise seemed to be okay.

Maggie slid in the backseat beside me and Chris took the one in front so he could lean over us. After digging through the piles of junk in her book bag, she pulled out a box wrapped in the Sunday funnies and tossed it in my lap. "Happy Birthday, dummy. I hope you like them."

After yanking the paper off, a long white box was revealed. Inside that box was a pair of navy blue suede low top Converse tennis shoes. Maggie had taken out the plain white shoestrings they came with and replaced them with my favorite color-lime green. "Oh! Oh!" Was all I could get out I was so excited. I had admired these shoes a hundred times and could never talk my mom into getting them. "I love you-forever. "

"Ewe. Don't be all weird and mushy about it,

18

you're giving me the creeps. Just put them on. And you're welcome."

I was tying up the new shoes and cramming the old smelly pair in my book bag just as we pulled up to the front door of Vernon High School where I was a sophomore.

Life was looking up for a change. I was officially sixteen, had a cool new pair of shoes, had an invite to what was shaping up to be an awesome party and later on I was going to ace my driving test and get my first true taste of independence.

What could possibly go wrong?

4 MILLIE AND THE DMV

As it turns out, a lot of crap can go wrong when you're me.

There are people out there who somehow manage to live their lives flawlessly. It's like they come out of the womb with an instruction manual in their hand that gives them an advantage where not screwing up is concerned.

Then, there are people like me who come out of the womb in the backseat of puke green Chrysler Cordoba. My mom said I was supposed to be born in a hospital, but they never made it. Every time she tells the story I cringe.

"We were halfway there when I kept hearing these giggling noises. George pulled over to investigate and it just happened that when he put our luggage in the trunk he was so excited he threw

your brother in along with the suitcase. By the time we talked him out of the trunk, you were on your way. That dad of yours can be a real idiot sometimes."

So, as you can see, my chances of ever being normal were practically slim to none from the get-go.

And as far as I can tell, I never got any kind of a manual. I usually just call customer service direct and speak with the big manager in the sky via prayer.

I know he's a busy guy and all, but I'm convinced I get put on hold a lot more than most people. I spend a lot of time listening to dead air and it gets a little aggravating, but I don't plan to stop trying to get through.

I'm just hoping I don't go overboard and make the good Lord mad with my constant complaining. It would be awful if he up and decided to cancel my service.

Today, however, is special. I'm going to need customer service, technical support and quite possibly a personal visit from the boss himself if I want to pass my driver's test. I don't do well when nerves are involved, so it'd be nice to have the backup.

It would also be nice if I had an actual car of my own. I was hoping this would happen sooner rather than later, but it was looking to be a few more months away until I saved up enough to actually buy one.

My mom and dad promised to match my funds when I had a decent amount put back, so I'd taken on a part time job at Big Daddy's Doughnuts as the Dancing Doughnut Girl.

I tried getting a job at a place that sells CD's or clothes. You know, something not nerdy or embarrassing. But, as fate would have it, all the good jobs were taken and I needed one fast.

Without any other options, I took what I could get and I am now forced to spend a few hours of my day, three days a week, handing out coupons in a big pink doughnut costume on the side of the road.

You will never know how hard it is to do the Roger Rabbit while wearing shoes shaped like doughnut holes until you've tried it yourself. Every time you fall down (which happens often) one of the 'sprinkles' falls off and you're one cotton ball closer to getting canned.

I hate that damn doughnut.

Thankfully, my dad was on time and showed up to get me from school at one o'clock sharp just like he'd promised. We made it to the DMV just in time for the last round of testing for the day. We were told to wait on a bench outside until they called for me.

My dad is notorious for his lectures about safety. If you leave a sock near a furnace vent or dare to carelessly yank a cord out of a wall outlet, you're bound to get a good talking to. Now that I am about get a driver's license, Captain Safety is out in full force.

"Millie, I know you're probably tired of hearing it, but you have got to promise me that you will drive

22

responsibly. If you drink and drive, your mother and I will kill you. If you go parking, we will kill you. If you get a ticket, we will put you to work cleaning up our hoarder from hell cousin Earl's house to pay for it. Am I making myself clear? "

I was shaking my head up and down in an attempt to agree, but couldn't do anything more than that because his threat was genuinely scary. Our cousin Earl had some serious issues in the housekeeping department and just the thought of going in his yard made me feel squicky. The guy kept everything.

My mom took my brother and I there once while she delivered some groceries. I got lost in a pile of plastic coat hangers and it took my mom twenty minutes to dig me out. We found my brother in the corner of an upstairs bedroom talking to a pile of dryer lint that he'd mistaken for Earl's cat.

We never went back.

I was still having Earl flash backs when a short, squatty little bald man poked his head around the door of the office and called my name.

"Wish me luck!"

My license evaluator looked to be in his mid-40's or so and was wearing a pair of wrinkled dress pants and a bright yellow button up shirt. He checked my eyes, gave me a quick written test (which I passed with flying colors, thank you very much) and we went outside to the car.

Before getting in, he stood and paused at his open door. "My name is Mr. Spinner. You're Millicent May Crantz, age sixteen, and this is your first attempt at a driver's license, correct?"

I nodded my head at him across the roof of the car. "Yes, sir! But can you call me Millie? People only call me Millicent when I'm in trouble and it makes me nervous."

Looking at me over the tops of a pair of wire rimmed glasses that were too small for his face, he regarded me for a minute before he shot out a very hateful, "No." Then, as if he wasn't the rudest little man in Kentucky, sat down and shut the door.

This should be fun; like a lobotomy-only more painful.

I got in the driver's seat and made sure to make a big production out of putting on my seatbelt while he was fiddling with his clipboard. Captain Safety would have been proud.

A wave of excitement washed over me as I started the car. This is it. I'm going to be a driver. I'll finally get to feel the wind whip through my hair and listen to the radio as loud as I want without someone telling me I was ruining my eardrums.

I didn't realize how spaced out I'd gotten until I noticed there was a clicking noise coming from somewhere. I opened my eyes to find Mr. Spinner snapping his fingers scarily close to my face.

"Okay, Miss Crantz. First, I need you to listen to all of my instructions and not do that spacing out thing you just did. "

Trying to pretend I was some kind of professional and hadn't just lapsed into my own personal head movie, I over excitedly and very dorkily squeaked out a, "Check!"

"Yes, glad you came back from La-La Land. Now, I want you to slowly back out of this parking spot and go straight up towards the stop sign at the end of street, then take a left. I'll tell you where to go from there."

I adjusted my rear view, put it in reverse and backed out. We were at the stop sign when I realized he was constantly putting some kind of mark on that clipboard of his.

How much could I have missed already? We'd only gone one block so far.

We tooled around the city for a little while. I was a nervous wreck over his constant clipboard doodling and ready to shove his pencil in a bad place when we finally came to the final part of the test, and my least favorite activity, parallel parking.

"That spot should do." He said as he nodded over to a place on the side of the street.

I gasped out loud. The place he'd chosen was the smallest space available in the whole city and was positioned between a Mercedes and a very expensive looking SUV.

"I can do this." I mumbled to myself.

What seemed like three hours and twelve gallons of sweat later, I was parked perfectly.

Take that little red faced man.

I was relearning to breathe when he turned suddenly and looked at me funny. "Excuse me?"

"What? I didn't say anything?" What a fruitcake. I think the stress of his job was getting to him.

"You did. Something about a red faced man?"

Crap. Had I said that out loud?

"Oh, um. I think I said *I needed a little rest now, man.* Like to relax for a second? That's what I said. Nothing about a red faced man! Why would I say something like that? Who has a red face? Nobody, that's who! Well, an Oompa Loompa is kind of red, but mostly they're orange." I was now rambling incoherently.

I wouldn't have thought it possible, but the more I talked, the redder he got until I thought his head might explode. If I didn't know better, I'd think he didn't believe me.

Thankfully, he took a few deep breaths and gave a slight nod of the head to pull out.

By the time we got back to the courthouse and pulled into a parking space, I was sweating profusely and trying to come to terms with the fact that I had probably blown any chance I had of passing. I didn't was afraid to look at him.

"So," I said meekly still looking straight ahead. "Did I pass?"

I found enough courage to spare a glance at Mr. Spinner, expecting him to hand me my big old F-. Instead, he had his head lying on his chest and appeared to be asleep.

I lightly tapped his shoulder with my index finger and he didn't move. I yelled his name a few times while waving my hand in front of his face like a maniac and still got nothing. As a last resort I reached over and gave him a shake. The clipboard he was holding fell in the floor with a clang and his head banged against the window as if he was a rag doll.

"Holy crap! I've killed the driver's license guy!" I yelled to nobody in particular.

I then went into full on panic mode and tried to get out of the car with my seatbelt still buckled and almost strangled myself to death. Once I detangled myself I ran inside to get help.

After throwing open the glass front doors to the courthouse I was relieved to see a janitor standing just inside. I was out of breath and, in my haste to explain the situation, I didn't notice that he was mopping. As soon as my feet made contact with the slippery marble floor, my legs flew out from underneath of me and I landed square on my back with a thump.

Thanks to a nice dose of adrenaline, it didn't hurt right away, so I quickly told the janitor what happened and he immediately ran off to call 911.

Two minutes later as I was still trying to breathe through the panic attack I was having, I heard sirens. I went to find my dad and found him standing on the curb nearby, watching the emergency crews work on Mr. Spinner.

As soon as he saw me he grabbed me up in a hug so fierce that I was afraid he'd damaged my spleen. "You didn't do all of this, did you? Tell me that is someone else's license evaluator."

"It wasn't my fault. He just kind of died or something."

With a smile that looked both relieved and somewhat strained, he reached over and patted me on the head. "I love you dearly, kid. But truth be told, you have a serious knack for getting yourself in the most ridiculous situations."

I would be offended by that statement, but he's right. I really am a walking disaster.

After they loaded him on a stretcher and whisked him away in the ambulance, a stern looking policeman with a head of bushy grey hair and matching unibrow walked over to talk to us. His uniform shirt was stretched over a belly that had seen one or twenty beers in its day. "Hi, folks. I'm Officer Wells. Which one of you is Millicent May Crantz? I need a statement about what happened here today."

Was he for real? As if my dad actually looked like a Millicent?

"That's me," I said in a terrified whisper. My dad gave me a light pat on the back to comfort me, but it wasn't really helping.

"I swear it wasn't my fault! I was just driving and I noticed his face had turned red but I thought that was always how he looked. When we pulled in I asked him if I'd passed my test and I guess he'd died or fainted or something. Is he dead?"

If he was dead I was going to be in so much trouble. I'll spend the rest of my life on a bus sitting next to a lady that smells like soup.

Clearly enjoying his role as interrogator, Officer Wells smirked slightly and hiked his pants up by the belt that held his gun. "No, ma'am. Mr. Spinner has diabetes and a heart condition. According to coworkers, he skipped lunch today. The paramedics expect him to make a full recovery. They did find a large knot on the right side of his head, though. Any idea what happened there?"

Whoops. I guess I shook him a little too hard. "No, sir. Everything was fine up until he almost died."

Sure, it was a little white lie. But, seriously? Who would actually admit that they'd beaten an unconscious man's head against a car door? What would my mom say?

Satisfied by my answer, he shook my dad's hand and told us we could go home. I had no way of knowing whether or not I'd passed my test, which was a complete bummer. But, after the whole ordeal I wasn't too depressed about it. I was just glad to be going home without a murder charge hanging over my head.

Besides, I still had a party to go to and it was still my birthday. Why not enjoy what's left of it?

5 BIRTHDAY HELL

Pulling in the driveway of our family home was kind of comforting after my tango with Mr. Spinner. The two story brick house with its burgundy shutters and the matching front door with its big golden door knocker were modest, but no less beautiful.

My parents treated landscaping as if it was a fine art and not actual work. My mom's flowers were her version of the Mona Lisa and my dad's obsession with cutting grass was like watching Michelangelo paint the Sistine Chapel.

My particular yard duty involved picking up loose sticks and garbage to make sure my dad didn't run them over with the lawnmower. Every now and then I'd get lazy and miss a piece of trash and end up spending twice the amount of time picking up the miniscule pieces left after my dad ran it over with the lawnmower.

As we walked up the sidewalk to the front door, I noticed Mrs. Fallcheck had a lot of company, which was odd. Mrs. Fallcheck never had company. Actually, Mr. and Mrs. Holman across the street also seemed to be having a party?

Then, it hit me and I recognized my Aunt Verna's car sitting in the Fallcheck's driveway.

I knew it was hers because she was the only person I knew with a bumper sticker on the back that said I Love Boobies. Her ex-husband had stuck it on there years ago when they'd divorced and despite her best efforts, it wouldn't come off.

I stopped dead in my tracks in the middle of our front porch. My dad ran into the back of me and I turned around to give him the stink eye.

"What's going on? Why are all the neighbors having parties all of a sudden?"

The look on his face combined with his sudden case of the fidgets confirmed my suspicions. Behind that big red front door, my friends and family are waiting on me to walk in so they can surprise me with the birthday party that I never wanted.

My dad was clearly not looking forward to it either. But, if I know one thing for sure- when Earnestine Crantz wants something-she usually gets it.

My mom loves having people over for dinner, but I don't know why she bothers. Our family is well-known for our ability to turn a civilized dinner party into a horror movie.

She had Pastor Dan from our church over a few weekends ago to celebrate his birthday. Grandma Lucille turned our post prayer dinner conversation into a discussion about how when she was his age, she started having bladder control problems. She also gave him a birthday card filled with adult diaper coupons she'd clipped from the newspaper.

I don't know if the woman is a saint capable of mass amounts of forgiveness or she just uses the dinner parties as an excuse to hit the bottle afterwards.

With his second comforting pat on the shoulder of the evening, my dad was as resigned as I was. "Millie, just go in and get it over with."

I took a deep breath, pushed open the front door, gritted my teeth and tried not to look like I was just diagnosed with a terminal illness as I stepped across the threshold.

A very loud and synchronized, "Surprise!" followed and so began the excitement. I said a little prayer that I would come out of the ordeal with all my hair still intact.

The screams came from all sides of the entryway and were followed by a hilariously out of tune Happy Birthday. My family was quickly piling out of the kitchen to my left and my friends out of the living room to my right. I was immediately surrounded and had no clear route of escape.

The first person to reach me was my mom who grabbed me up in a big hug, gave me a kiss on the forehead and whispered, "Don't be mad. My only daughter turns sixteen just this once in both of our lifetimes, so I would like to celebrate it."

I nodded and smiled. I knew her intentions were good and love the woman dearly no matter what.

After practically shoving my mom out of the way, my Aunt Verna was the next to get a hold of me. As usual, she was dragging her husband Wally behind her like he was a stray puppy on a short leash.

Even though she was my mom's sister, they were complete opposites in every way. My mom was conservative with a fairly decent sense of humor and a logical way of thinking. My Aunt Verna, however, dressed like a Jersey housewife circa 1970 and was borderline obsessive compulsive with severe hypochondria.

Today she'd chosen a shiny gold and black tiger striped sweatshirt, black pants and enough jewelry to put a mobster's wife to shame. Her over-dyed blonde hair was piled up on her head in a gigantic wad and every time she walked under one of the ceiling fixtures I saw my dad flinch.

Letting go of poor Uncle Wally, she reached up and put a hand on each side of my face. "Oh, just look at you! You're getting so big now! Turn around here and let me have a look at you!"

Twirling around quickly to appease her, I badly wanted to remind her that she'd seen me just day before yesterday.

She gave me a very slow once over that made me extremely uncomfortable. "You know, I would have thought you'd take your boobs after your mom's side of the family. "

To illustrate the fact that all of my mom's family had overdeveloped chests, she stuck hers out and pointed to them. "Maybe you will eventually get a good pair. After all, you're still young, right? Never say never!"

I immediately started looking around for someone to help me out of the conversation and almost gave up when a very drunk Uncle Lou burst through the front door.

It was well known that Uncle Lou had a bit of a drinking problem, but he wasn't the kind of drunk everybody hated and was well loved by everyone in our family. He was a little over six foot tall and so skinny you could floss your teeth with him. He was wearing his trademark plaid shorts, brown moccasins with bright orange socks and a green t-shirt that had the phrase I'm A Freaking Genius scrawled across the front.

After handing me a bag that I assumed was a present, he slurred out a quick Happy Birthday and ambled into the dining room where everyone else was migrating for dinner.

"Dude. Your Uncle Lou is the coolest guy ever."

I looked behind me to find Maggie and Chris standing there with smiles on their faces, clearly enjoying my horror.

Maggie grabbed Uncle Lou's present out of my hand and took a peek. The range of emotions on her face went from shock, to awe and finally all out hilarity. She reached in and pulled out a mason jar that had some kind of clear liquid in it.

"What the heck is that?" I asked, grabbing it out of her hand. I turned it around so I could see the label, but was surprised to find that it was just a white piece of paper crudely taped to the jar with the word's Gen-u-wine Moonshine written on it in in black marker.

My Uncle Lou had gotten me a jar of illegally made moonshine for my sixteenth birthday. My mom was going to have a heart attack.

Still holding my fancy new booze, I smiled and said, "I should be mad at you guy's for not telling me about this. Lucky for you I'm in a good mood and looking forward to later. I just hope we aren't caught, tarred and then feathered. "

You see, I wasn't technically allowed to go to the party because my mom and dad insisted I was too young to be out gallivanting around town on a school night. However, after weeks of planning, Maggie and I had it all worked out.

I would sneak out of the house and go gallivanting anyways.

Our initial plan starred me as the driver, but after today's catastrophe, I had to give them a quick rundown of the day's events and explain why I couldn't do it. I was partly relieved because I'd had no idea how I was going to get out of my driveway with my mom's car without being heard.

After the obnoxious laughing and snorting subsided, we were able to get back to the topic at hand.

With an air of confidence that I didn't quite trust, Maggie did her best to calm me down. "It's okay, Mil. You just do your part and get out of here without getting caught. I'll handle the rest. I'll meet you at the corner of Lexington around midnight. "

Backing her up like a champ, Chris piped in with a cheerful, "You'll be fine, Mil! I'll meet you all there and we'll all be fine!"

Easy for him to say. He was allowed to go and didn't have to pull a James Bond to get out of his house.

"You all better be right." I said, not believing in the slightest that any of this was going to work out in my favor.

Plans made, they left and I went into the dining room to face the familial music. I sat the moonshine down in front of my dad who did a double take before looking over at Lou with a frown. He mumbled a few curse words and stuck it in the China cabinet that sat right behind his usual chair.

The family dining room was pretty big and comfortably sat all eight of us. The good China was out and the little pink roses on the place settings complimented the mint green walls just as my mom had intended.

My Grandma Lucille always sat right next to me (which was as far away from my dad as we could get her) and my brother was always on the other side of her. Mom and dad sat at the opposite ends of the table and Uncle Lou, Uncle Wally and Aunt Lucille sat across from us.

My mom made spaghetti since it was my favorite and we all passed around plates to serve ourselves. For a few minutes, all was quiet aside from the clank of dishes being scraped with forks and glasses being filled.

The only thing in the world capable of silencing a Crantz is a good meal.

While I hadn't noticed it when I walked in, my dad had installed a new ceiling fan in the dining room at some point and the force of the air coming from it was so strong it was ruffling up the napkins, causing mine to fly all over the place. I looked over to see if anybody else was having problems and realized Grandma Lucille was staring a hole in Uncle Wally's head.

Wally is the walking, talking definition of nerd. He's short, extremely thin, very pale and wears glasses so thick they magnify his eyes and make them look entirely too big for his face. He was also in denial about his hair loss and had an extremely bad comb-over that was basically just a few long hairs he'd grown out, combed to the side and then anchored down with mass amounts of hairspray.

Due to what I believe was just bad luck on Wally's part, he happened to be sitting opposite the direction of the flow of air coming down from the new fan. The wind it created had somehow crept underneath the side of his comb over and lifted it straight up in the air.

I chuckled as quietly as I could and was surprised to see that nobody else besides me and grandma had noticed it.

Grandma Lucille, however, made sure she brought it to everyone's attention.

"Why, look there at that man's hair," She said pointing in Wally's direction. "I don't know if he's waving at me or taking the top off his candy dish to offer me a peppermint."

My mom choked on a mouthful of pasta and my dad laughed until the veins on his face were popping out. My brother didn't really notice because he was too busy carefully placing spaghetti noodles on a sleeping Uncle Lou's face.

Aunt Verna dug a bobby pin out of her purse and discreetly handed it to Wally while giving us all dirty looks.

My mom, ever the peacekeeper, decided that was a good time to bring out the cake and disappeared into the kitchen. She emerged a few minutes later, cake in hand and a strained smile on her face. She came over to my side of the table and mouthed, "I'm sorry" before she he sat the cake down in front of me.

Why is she apologizing?

I looked down at the cake, confused. The first thing I noticed were the two lit candles, a one and a six that represented my age. The second thing I noticed was that the cake was decorated with characters from Scooby Doo, a favorite cartoon of mine since I can remember.

I was pondering my mom's decision to get a Scooby Doo themed birthday cake for a sixteen year old when I noticed that the entire Mystery Gang had been rearranged and appeared to be enjoying one another's company in a very adult way.

Grandma Lucille gasped. "Well, look there at them little plastic folks doing their little plastic pervert deeds on that cake! I never seen one like that! That is just fancy!"

My Uncle Wally chimed in, "It looks like Scooby is turning tricks to earn his Scooby Snacks." Aunt Verna gave him a girly slap in the arm and started to giggle.

After absorbing the shock, the entire family started laughing hysterically. The noise was enough to pull Uncle Lou out of his stupor and he sat up slightly in his chair looking startled, but oblivious to the fact that his face was covered in noodles-which were now falling into his lap one by one.

He looked at the cake, smiled knowingly and with slurred enthusiasm said, "Happy Birthday, Molly!" before passing back out again.

Molly?

6 SNEAKIN' OUT AND FREAKIN' OUT

Sneaking out of the house isn't just risky, it's downright stupid. I hadn't ever entertained the idea until now, but I had to get to Eva's party. For once in my life, I was going to do something that wasn't safe-- something badass. This was my chance.

Every nerve ending in my entire body was tingling in fear and apprehension. If I screw this up, I might never be able to go outside again. Even worse, my dad will make good on his promise and send me to Uncle Earl's house; never to be seen from or heard from again--lost forever in a pile of old paperclips and Beanie Babies.

Since I had plenty of time to prepare myself while I waited on my mom and dad to go to bed, I took my time getting ready. I put on the one pair jeans that I thought made my butt look good and spent at least twenty minutes craning my neck around to look at it in the mirror. I decided they would work and threw on a white tank top with a blue and grey checked flannel shirt that would match my new shoes. I spent a little extra time trying to tame down my curly afro, put on my makeup a little heavier than usual and was ready to go.

I'd already decided that the window beside the couch in the living room was my best option for a quiet getaway. It's low enough that I can reach it, but big enough to squeeze through.

I sent up a small prayer and asked God to not let me get stuck while trying to climb out. Probably it's not right to ask God for permission to break one of the Ten Commandments. But, I'm desperate. Desperate people do desperate stuff all the time.

I tip toed past my mom and dad's room. Their door was shut, but they both snore like there's no tomorrow, so I could tell they were down for the count. It sounded like a monster truck rally was going on in there.

The entire house was pitch black at night, so navigating my way around furniture wasn't very easy. With a deep breath I started making my way through the house, breathing only when absolutely necessary. I was doing my best to avoid making any noise, but our house is kind of old and things creak and rattle no matter how hard you try.

I didn't hesitate when I got to the window. I immediately flipped the lock and, very delicately, started to lift it. Every centimeter that window lifted put me a centimeter closer to my freedom. Every time it groaned in protest I was in danger of losing that freedom for the rest of my natural born life.

Finally, after what seemed like twenty years, I had it open as far as it would go. I hopped up and pushed myself through. My butt got a little jammed, just barely making it through the tiny opening. I scuffed both of my hips and a boob, but I made it.

As soon as my feet hit the ground I ran like hell.

I was so preoccupied, worried that any minute my mom would pop out of the house in her nightgown and curlers to chase after me that I ran straight into a big blue post office box and was knocked backwards onto the ground. I scraped both elbows and landed on my butt hard enough that I now know what my tailbone tastes like.

With a sigh and some silent curses, I got up and dusted myself off. I was surveying the fresh cuts and bruises on my arms when I noticed that my neighborhood, normally warm and welcoming in the daytime, had a more sinister feel in the dark.

"Don't be a wuss, Millie. People are asleep this time of night." I said out loud to nobody in particular.

The Kellerman's live a little ways down the street from us on the corner and have a pit-bull named Minnie who, contrary to what her name implies, is the size of a house. She barked and I almost jumped inside the letter slot of the mailbox I'd just run into.

I made a mental note to check my underpants before we went to the party.

"Stupid dog."

A set of headlights whipped past me and I tensed up. As a car rounded the curve at the head of the street my mind started to race with the possibilities of who, or what, might be in that car.

What if it wasn't Maggie? What if it was a rapist out to get little girls who sneak out and defy their parents? What if that rapist has a hatchet?

The car slowed and I started backing up. Maybe this isn't such a good idea, I thought. Probably I should go home and go back to bed. My school pictures never turned out very good. They'd look awful on a milk carton.

Pulling to a stop in front of me, the window was rolled down and, to my relief Maggie yelled, "You made it! Get in!"

After a few seconds of letting my eyes adjust to the familiarity of Maggie's features and the outline of the red Volkswagen Jetta she drove, I started to relax and felt the blood slowly start creeping back up into my face.

Noticing my apparent panic, Maggie looked suddenly concerned. "Whoa! What in the hell is the matter with you? You look like you're about ready to cry!"

I don't know how she makes everything look so easy. I hate her sometimes.

"I'm so glad you're not a rape artist." I said, opening the door and sliding into the seat next to her.

"A rape artist? I don't even know what that is?" She said with a grin. She knew this sneaking around was freaking me out. I'm so glad she found it humorous.

The jerk.

"Yeah, you know, a sleazy dude with scraggly chin hair and great big pedophile glasses? Quit laughing at me. I'm nervous."

"Please. You're such a drama queen. Calm down."

"I just broke out of Crantz Federal Penitentiary. You wouldn't be so calm if you thought my mom was after you."

"You're right, I wouldn't. When her eyes get all wide and glow green I know to run for the hills. Your mom is scary when she's mad."

"Tell me about it."

When Maggie stopped making fun of me and conversation stopped all together, I started thinking about what we were doing. I could see the yellow lines on the road disappearing under the car and felt my excitement level ratchet up a notch, soothing my nervous stomach. Maggie turned the radio up and the soft, mellow sounds of Radiohead's Karma Police drifted through the car.

I rolled down the window and stuck my head out, feeling the cool breeze of the night air whip my hair around my face. It's the first time I've ever been bold enough to do something so rebellious and at that very moment, it felt really good to be me.

It's also the first time I've ever swallowed an entire moth. Next time I'll remember to keep my mouth closed.

Gross.

After five or so minutes on the road (and a lot of gagging and telling Maggie to shut-up over the bug thing), we pulled over to the side of the road on a small street just a couple blocks from my own house. Maggie turned on the overhead light and adjusted her makeup in the rearview. She then swiveled her body in my direction and looked at me like she was waiting for something.

"What? Why are you looking at me?"

"We're here. Turner Street. Now, which house is it?"

"What? I don't know. I thought you knew? How would I know? I didn't come up with this plan, you did. "

I should have known better than to involve myself in this cockamamie scheme. Maggie's plans were never very well laid out. I was going to get caught and later, after I was fifty four and allowed out of my house again, I would kill her.

"No, you said you knew which house! I don't know which house I just know the street."

After carefully considering our options, I said, "Well, it can't be that hard. There are what, five houses? Look, there's only one there with the lights on. We'll park here and walk up. It's a party. If it's the right house we should be able to see it through the window, right?

"Makes sense to me." Maggie was ever the optimist.

Slowly and carefully, we exited the car. I shut my door quietly but Maggie slammed hers, making noise that people three blocks over could probably hear.

"Do you mind? We're trying to be stealthy. I don't want half the city coming out thinking we're being bombed!"

"Would you come on already?"

After double checking the outfit, eyeing the makeup and fluffing my hair in the side view mirror, I started towards the house. I was going to that party no matter what happened. I didn't give myself three heart attacks, two severely scraped elbows and a damaged boob for nothing.

"Let's go." I sounded more badass than I felt.

The house was smack in the middle of a cookie cutter neighborhood, all one story brick ranch homes with attached garages. There was a fountain in the front yard of this particular house. The little boy was spitting a steady stream of water into the pool below his feet, making a subtle splashing sound that was comforting. It also brought about the need for a restroom break.

As we approached the front porch, we could hear music pounding from inside. This had to be the right house.

Slowly climbing the steps, we stooped down in front of a large picture window, lifting our heads just enough to look into what looked like the living room.

It wasn't the party. Well, not the party we were looking for anyways.

"What in the hell—?" Maggie whispered, her face frozen in a grimace.

I could barely hear what she was saying. Whoever was throwing this party was playing Madonna's Like a Virgin so loud that the glass in the windows rattled.

"Is that Mr. Bostick?" I asked, trying my best to make sense out of what I was seeing.

"You mean Mrs. Bostick?"

"No, I mean Mr."

My brain just stopped working all together for a few seconds. I don't know if it was a self-defense thing or just shock that had rendered me speechless.

Mr. Bostick, our elementary school principal, was standing in front of a full length mirror applying a fresh coat of fire engine red lipstick to his seventy five year old lips.

This guy had been putting the fear of God in students at Grant Elementary School for the last twelve thousand years. I hadn't ever seen him in anything but a wool suit jacket, his signature brown wingtips and a white button up shirt that always had coffee dribble stains down the front. He was normally bald, but tonight he was Dolly Parton blonde thanks to the shoulder length wig he had on, which was lopsided and poorly combed.

Mr. Bostick has always been a big man--big belly, big head-big everything; but his legs were the size of toothpicks and I always wondered how they held the top of him up. He was sashaying around in front of that mirror like he was Buffalo Bill, all done up in a red lace teddy, fish net tights and four inch hooker pumps.

The teddy was so sheer you could see Principal Bostick's seventy five year old everything. His legs were clearly doing their job but I couldn't say the same for the rest of him. I've never seen so many wrinkles in one place.

"You know how when you pass a car wreck and look to see if there's a dead body or decapitated head rolling around? You don't really want to see it, but you look anyways?" Maggie said with an involuntary shiver, "That's what this is like. I'm ashamed of myself but I keep looking at Bostick's

Willis and Doodle berries. I don't want to see them, but it's impossible to look away."

"Thank you for telling me. Now I can't quit looking at his Willis and Doodle berries. We need to leave. I'm going to take a scrub brush to my brain when we get home."

We were getting ready to leave and put this whole nightmare behind us when Mr. Bostick turned and seemingly looked straight at us. We crouched below the window frame and got down as low as our bodies and the front porch would allow.

"We should go." I whispered as low as humanly possible. "It's going to be really embarrassing if we are arrested for being peeping toms that spy on cross dressing principals. Besides, I reached my What the Hell quota for today when the DMV guy did that almost dying thing."

Maggie's face was pinched with held back laughter. "Okay, yeah. I need to go have a lobotomy later anyways. Or counseling. Or both maybe."

We were making our way down the stairs, both of us doing our best impressions of a slow motion playback so as not to be noisy, when a car turned the corner at the end of the street. Taking immediate action, Maggie jumped down all four steps and darted around the house. Not able to think nearly as quickly as her, I stupidly jumped into the bushes that trimmed the front porch.

And what do you know? I'd jumped into rose bushes. It felt like I'd leapt into a pile of thumb tacks. Why couldn't it have been dandelions? Or a pillow tree?

As the car started to slow I realized it was headed straight for us. I could feel my heart beating in my ears, I still needed a bathroom because of that tacky fountain and now I had an ass full of thorns.

The car pulled into the driveway and came to a stop. The driver's side door opened and through the branches of my not at all awesome hiding place I saw a long, panty hose covered leg with a six inch heel attached plant itself on the driveway with a clack. This was followed by another heel and finally, an entire person.

She was at least six foot tall, had a head of billboard sized red hair and boobs for miles. She certainly wasn't there to sell Avon. I'm pretty sure the Avon lady doesn't sell eye shadow in a black pleather bustier and spandex skirt. This lady was a professional.

She sauntered up the sidewalk and as she started up the steps beside me, I could hear the creaks and groans her outfit made as she moved. It sounded like somebody was making balloon animals.

She hit the doorbell and started riffling through her humongous bag. After a long search, she pulled out a compact and dutifully checked her makeup and hair while she waited on someone to answer. I had a sudden urge to yell out a warning and let her know Mr.

Bostick was running around with his business all over the place, but I didn't think she would care.

Swinging the door wide open with an enthusiastic grin and clearly unashamed by the fact that his doodles were on display, Mr. Bostick greeted the lady with a familiar embrace. "Darla! You look fabulous! Come on in!"

I shuddered. Just thinking about that man hugging me in the state he was in absolutely terrified me.

"Leroy, you look to die for in that teddy!" Darla said as she walked into the house. The rest of their conversation faded away as they both disappeared behind the door.

Maggie emerged from her hiding place at the side of the house and I, ungracefully, pulled myself free of the rosebush I'd landed in. I rubbed my hands over my face, checking for any thorns that may be sticking out of my forehead.

"Who was that?" I asked Maggie, picking leaves out of my hair.

"Darla? I have no idea. Is it weird that I want to go back up there and see?"

"You can't be serious. I don't even know if I can be your friend anymore with talk like that. You need to call a crisis hotline or have some intensive electroshock therapy. That's just sick."

"I even agree with you there and yet, still…"

After lingering in the yard for a few minutes while Maggie had an internal war with herself about eavesdropping on monumental grossness, we finally left and went back to the car.

We both got in, threw on our seatbelts and Maggie asked, "Okay, where to then?"

"I don't know." I was disappointed about the party and ready to go home. "I say we just head home and forget this ever happened."

"Okay" she replied, looking as down as I felt. "This is crap. What a waste of a good evening."

She put the car in drive and pulled out. I was kind of relieved to be going home because at this point, my paranoia was starting to eat at me in a bad way and had sucked all of the exciting out of it.

Plus, I'd just been visually assaulted by an old man and his bits and pieces, so that didn't help much either.

I was sitting quietly, thinking about the day I'd had and watching the trees and houses whiz by my window when out of nowhere, Maggie started screaming bloody murder and slammed on the breaks.

I heard a thump at the front of the car and braced myself on the dashboard to keep from hitting my head on it. I was thrust forward so hard that the coarse material of my seatbelt burnt my neck.

After giving her a quick once over to assess her for gushing head wounds and broken bones, I started to yell.

"What-are-you-doing! What just happened?"

Looking back over at her, I realized that I was the only one talking and Maggie's eyes were wide and focused on a lump in the road that was just beyond the reach of the headlights. My heart started pounding and I could already feel the beads of sweat forming on my forehead.

Had we hit somebody?

We both took off our seatbelts and stepped out of the car. Maggie left it running, so we had enough light from the headlights to get a good look at what was going on. I glanced at the front of Maggie's car as we walked by it and was pleased to note that it didn't sustain any damage.

That was a small comfort considering the fact that I was about ready to throw up. If there was a dead, semi-dead or seriously injured person up there we were screwed.

How many people were going to almost die today?

Inching closer, I saw a hoof and breathed a sigh of relief. It wasn't a person, it was a deer.

"Awe, look at that poor thing!" I said sadly.

"Do you think it's dead?" Maggie asked.

"I'm pretty sure it's dead. Well, I mean I think it's dead? Check its pulse or something."

"What? I don't want to touch it! What if it bites me? You touch it!" She stood there looking at me incredulously as if deer were known for their aggressive natures and might eat her alive if she got too close.

"Well, you hit it! I don't want to touch it. I try not to touch dead things. It's a rule I have."

A couple of minutes went by before she wondered over to one of the trees lining the road, snapped a branch off one of them and shucked off the leaves.

As I frowned at her with disapproval, she walked over to the deer and started lightly poking it with her stick. Nothing happened.

"Yep, it's dead. What do we do?"

"You sure it's dead, Dr. Maggie? How can you tell by just rudely jabbing it with a stick?"

She crinkled her face up at me, clearly aggravated that I was being sarcastic. "You got a better idea? Quit being a smartass and just help me move it."

Knowing I had to get home sometime before my next birthday, I relented even though I felt like this was a bad idea. "Fine. But you go get that end and I'll get this one." I said, pointing to the deer's back end. "Why do I get its butt?"
"Just go get it!"
"Fine."

Maggie grabbed the back legs and I grabbed the front. On the count of three, we started to lift.

As if lightening had come from the sky to revive it, the deer started to struggle. Maggie screamed, I said a word that would see me grounded or worse, and both of us ran back to the car as quick as our legs would carry us. I got so nervous I accidently got in the back seat instead of the front.

"Did you see that?" Maggie asked breathlessly.

Was she serious?

"What? You mean did I see the miracle deer come back to life? No, I must have missed that. Stupid!"

Maggie started laughing and I couldn't help but join her. This evening couldn't possibly get any stranger than it already had.

Once I'd caught my breath, I crawled back up into the front seat where I belonged and we finally made our way back to my house. And, believe it or not, we got there without killing ourselves or anyone else.

I even made it back in my house quietly.

As soon as I got in my room I kicked off my shoes and practically threw myself in bed, not even bothering with pajamas. I was out before my head hit the pillow.

This has been the longest birthday ever.

7 THIS IS NOT A DREAM

It seemed as though I'd just fallen asleep when I was yanked from my peaceful slumber by an extremely loud noise that sounded a whole lot like somebody was driving a train through my room.

My late night hadn't done me any favors and the sun coming in from my window was so bright that I could see it through my eyelids. I tried yelling for someone to knock of the racket when I realized that the sound was getting louder-and closer.

My eyes flew open and I sat up in a panic, looking around to see what was going on. My vision was blurry at first and the only thing I immediately recognized was a bunch of trees.

Trees?

I rubbed my eyes and stood up to get a better look at what was going on around me.

I was right about the trees, but wrong about the source of the noise. Nobody was driving a train through my room because I wasn't even IN my room. I was in the cemetery and had apparently fallen asleep here.

Ewe. I'd just taken a nap in the cemetery? Who the hell takes naps in cemeteries?

I looked down at my clothes and, even though the rain had stopped, they were still damp and sticking to me like wet newspaper. The sun had caused the patches of mud on my exposed legs to dry and crack, making it look like I had some kind of skin problem.

The noise was coming from a small crane in front of me that was lowering the casket down into its final resting place. There were two men standing on either side of the open grave helping the man working the crane guide the cargo into the ground.

Well, this is just downright awkward. How am I going to explain myself on this one? And how do three men not notice a woman covered in mud taking a nap by an open grave? Could they not have woken me up?

I couldn't help but stare at them while they worked. They were, after all, putting a dead person into the ground and didn't seem to notice me. If they did notice me, they certainly didn't acknowledge me.

That probably isn't a bad thing considering what I look like at the moment.

As soon as the casket itself was placed inside, the straps that held it were unhooked by a man who practically climbed in the grave to get to them. The crane was driven away and a backhoe was started to my left, just out of my line of sight. I jumped at the sound and felt a few of the dirt clods stuck to my legs fall off.

This isn't how it happens in the movies. In the movies, people throw in handfuls of dirt in while the coffin is lowered, say something dramatic and afterwards a creepy, yet loveable caretaker finishes up the task with a shovel--not heavy machinery.

I wonder? Can you request shovels and dramatic quotes be used at your own funeral? The thought of three strange men dangling me over a hole, dumping large buckets of dirt on me and then stomping on my grave just seems kind of tacky to me. I need to make a mental note to look into that later.

Once I stepped back into reality, I was surprised to find that the men were leaving and didn't so much as look in my direction the whole time they were here. But, I guess they see a lot of strange behavior from people in their line of work.

Also, it could be the fact that I look like a lunatic.

The thing is, I don't think I AM a lunatic. I feel kind of lost and like I'm supposed to be here all at the same time, but I don't know why.

Thinking back, I can't remember exactly how I got here, only that I was running late and just barely made it on time. I remember walking up to the crowd and feeling an overwhelming sense of loss that I didn't understand. My heart was telling me that the person inside the coffin was someone important to me, someone I loved, but my mind couldn't quite remember who.

I still feel that loss when I look at the now freshly covered grave and the feeling is so strong that I felt my breath catch a little. No matter my confusion or my circumstances, I am sure of one thing—something in my world has gone terribly wrong.

Maybe I have amnesia? I don't remember hitting my head, but it's certainly possible when you consider my lack of coordination.

If all of that isn't enough to mess a girl up, who was the sassy old lady with the shoes? My Fairy Rudemother, maybe?

I walked over to the freshly turned earth and sat cross-legged at its edge. The flowers had been laid along the length and there were so many you could barely make out the dirt beneath them. I made a quick check to see if there was a name marker left, but there wasn't.

Figures. That would be too easy.

"Who are you?" I whispered, hoping maybe whoever it was would sit up and just tell me already.

"Look at me!" I yelled at the ground. "I'm dirty, I'm tired, I'm confused and I'm talking to dead people. I could use some help here. Have I done something wrong? Am I an extra on the Twilight Zone and forgot?"

It goes without saying that I didn't get a reply. Last I checked, dead folks aren't big on conversations.

Without anywhere else to go or anything else to say, I started to cry. I tried to hold it back, but I couldn't. I let the full force of all the sorrow, anger and confusion I'd been feeling overwhelm me and my quiet sobs quickly became worse until I didn't think I could breathe.

Anger won out above all the others and I flew into a rage. I grabbed at the flowers and immediately began to tear them to shreds, ripping the petals from their stems and oblivious to the thorns drawing blood on my arms.

Then I started to scream. I screamed so loud and so long that it hurt. I banged my arms into the dirt until they were bruised and muddy and finally, I just gave up and collapsed.

Exhausted both physically and mentally, I laid there in the mess I'd made, quiet but still crying. I don't know if I fell asleep or just passed out, but the last thing I thought as I closed my eyes was that I didn't deserve this.

So why is it happening to me?

8 AMEN!

As you get older, life gets a whole lot more complicated. That whole 'older and wiser' mantra you hear so much as a kid is a big bunch of bull pocky if you ask me.

Life experience, the good and the bad, has a tendency to make you overthink things-even the small stuff. You develop a habit of making simple situations complicated and complicated situations damn near impossible, simply because you have a better grasp on the possible outcomes of those situations.

I think the decision making part of my brain was somehow damaged at birth. I was, after all, born in the backseat of a Cordoba. Maybe I inhaled too many exhaust fumes?

I felt a bony elbow bump my shoulder and came back from Planet Millie to see that it was my brother, George Jr., who'd done the elbowing. I shot him a dirty look and resisted the urge to smack him because we were in church. My mom would smack us both if we started a fist fight in a church pew.

I glanced up to see that Pastor Dan had only reached the middle of his sermon and sighed. I love Jesus as much as the next southern girl, but Pastor Dan's sermons were extremely boring. It was like watching a foreign film without the subtitles.

Our church was one of the biggest and oldest of the many we had here in Flatwoods. The congregation was made up of mostly what Grandma Lucille called "Old Flatwoods families." Everyone knew everyone else here and even though pews weren't assigned, they may as well have been. Not a Sunday went by that you didn't see the Crantz family in the third row.

Unfortunately, all of that togetherness led to a lot of very non-churchlike gossip. Just last week Mary Lou Botts brought Pastor Dan an extra container of baked beans for the church potluck and the next day's rumor was that they were having an affair.

The thing is, Mary Lou Botts is in her 90's and doesn't look to be in any kind of shape to be doing anything of the sort. She uses a walker 24/7 and sometimes she falls asleep during the sermon.

My mom, dad, brother, Grandma Lucille, Uncle Wally and Aunt Verna were all dressed in our church finery and sitting in a little row. Somehow I'd gotten stuck by my brother this go round and no matter how many subtle 'knock it off' looks I threw at him, he was still elbowing me.

I finally gave up and looked down at whatever it was he had in his hand. It was white, oblong and about the size of my pinkie finger, only much thinner. I couldn't tell what it was until he turned it over and I was able to read the generic label stamped on it that just said Ammonia Inhalant.

I was just about ready to ask him why he had it when he cracked open the package. The smell slammed into my nose like a Mac truck and I gagged a little. No wonder they use those things to wake up unconscious people. They're strong enough to wake the dead.

My dad was sitting on the other side of George silently reading a hymnal, so I figured it was only a matter of time until he smelled it and George was toast.

I waited for a second, but noticed that my dad wasn't turning the pages of his book and when I leaned over a little further to look at it, saw that it was actually upside down.

He was asleep.

Meanwhile, George had managed to wiggle the entire inhalant out of the package and the smell was getting more intense by the second. I tried discreetly slapping it out of his hand, but he jerked away so fast I missed him. That's when he made his move.

I was trying to decide what I could do to stop him and not draw attention to us, but I was too late. He'd already made his move.

His body shaking all over with soundless giggles, George stuck the inhalant directly under my dad's nose.

My dad was immediately roused from his sleep and jolted upright. He'd been slouching, but was so startled by the smell he went forward too fast and the momentum caused him to bang his head on the church pew in front of him. The crack of head hitting oak echoed off the walls of the church and my very confused dad yelled out a random, "Amen!"

While I must admit that George's prank was creative (and hilarious), I had no intention of taking the blame for his stupidity. Everyone in the church was now staring at us and I felt all the color drain out of my face when I saw that my mom was staring the hardest of all.

"He did it!" I said, pointing at George.

Taking mercy on us, Pastor Dan got back to his sermon and the attention of the crowd was diverted back onto him. My mom leaned over and whispered something in my brother's ear that caused his face to freeze in a horror.

She didn't think anybody noticed, but I saw Grandma Lucille give George Jr. a very discreet thumbs up before turning her attention back to the sermon.

9 WHAT JUST HAPPENED?

After church, the whole family goes back home for an early dinner and what my mom calls necessary family bonding time.

I always looked forward to the food portion of these meals because my mom was known all over town for her cooking. She went all out on Sundays and we always had the best of everything. Today's menu was no exception—chicken and dumplings, mashed potatoes, gravy, corn, green beans, sweet potato casserole and for dessert, a chocolate cake with fluffy white icing.

I helped set the table and put out eight settings like I usually do. All of the men were slowly piling in the dining room and taking their regular seats while my mom, Aunt Verna and Grandma Lucille finished up dinner.

My Uncle Lou was the only one missing from the group and I wondered where he was. That thought was quickly pushed aside when they started setting the food out on the table. I was starving.

"Where's that brother of mine at today?" Grandma Lucille asked as she laid a bowl of corn on the table? "He's usually here. That horse's ass is the biggest food eating freeloader this side of the Ohio River. I'm worried about him not showing up."

My mom noticed the absence then and you could tell she was also worried, but Uncle Lou wasn't exactly a dependable kind of guy, so I don't know why everyone was so concerned. It wasn't the first time he'd been tardy and certainly wouldn't be the last.

My mom went into the kitchen to call him and we all sat down and started eating. Her quick return and the look of strain on her face said Uncle Lou didn't answer.

Just as she started to sit down, my mom looked around the table and as if it was a huge faux pas, jumped up and said, "Oh! I forgot the wine!"

"I'll get it!" I said, pushing my chair back. The woman rarely ever ate a hot meal and between her constant cooking, worrying about guests and dealing with them as well—she deserved just a minute. The least I could do is get the wine.

I wouldn't mind a drink or two myself, but that wasn't going to happen anytime soon.

As I opened the door that leads from the kitchen to the garage, I was shocked to see that my mom had left the garage door open when she parked her car.

This was strange only because my mom was convinced that an open garage door detracted from the beauty of the house and insisted that it be closed at all times.

Preoccupied, I started to walk forward to hit the garage door button to close it but tripped over top of something blocking my path and ended up pushing the button with my face, not my hand like I intended.

My curse was thankfully muffled by the sound of the garage door mechanism but it didn't take long for me to realize that if I didn't get to the lights soon I was about to be lost in the dark. The garage was creepy in the dark.

Racing against the door, I ran back over and hit the lights. Once my eyes adjusted and I was able to orient myself, I set my sights on the fridge.

I walked around the edge of my mom's car and was headed for the wine when I saw the thing I'd tripped over on my way in. It was a very drunk, very passed out Uncle Lou. He was lying right in front of the door, face down and splayed out in a very unnatural position.

"Hey!" I yelled through the wall. "I found Uncle Lou! He's drunk and passed out in here!"

To make sure I snapped them from their feeding frenzy and was heard, I banged on the wall separating us and repeated myself.

I knew they'd gotten the message when a thunderous roar of feet started heading my way. The kitchen door opened and the first one out was my

Grandma Lucille. She leaned through the doorway and looked down at her inebriated brother, used her foot to turn him over and almost fell down.

Uncle Lou was wearing a pair of plaid shorts hiked all the way up to his chin, knee socks that had pink kittens all over them and a sleeveless muscle shirt that said Beauty is in the Eye of the Beerholder on the front.

My grandma Lucille bent down and just stared at him for a minute. "Look at that man. The drunkard. Them legs of his are so scrawny he looks like he's riding a chicken. I told our mother, God rest her soul, that he was a little touched in that head of his. Looks like I was right."

My mom gently pulled Grandma up and bent down to check on Lou. She put her ear down close to his mouth and checked his pulse. She repeated that process twice and I noticed her face getting a little whiter with each pass.

My dad was also getting concerned and worked his way through the back of the crowd. "What is it, Earnestine?"

He bent down and checked on Lou as well, but didn't say a word. He and my mom just kind of looked at each other for a few seconds and the quiet was all we needed.

Well, quiet would have been nice. When Grandma Lucille and Aunt Verna are around, this is hard to achieve

My Aunt Verna had also finally caught on. "Is he dead? If he's dead I will throw up!"

"Well, I'll be damned." Grandma Lucille added.

My mom jumped up and herded everyone back in the house and told us to go sit back down and try to eat while she called the ambulance.

"Ambulance? Earnestine, we ain't going to need no ambulance unless they got some kind of miracle cure for dead dummy that I never heard of. We need a hearse."

"Mom!" a tearful Aunt Verna yelled. "Don't be so awful! Your brother just died!"

It was the first time I've ever seen my Grandma Lucille look genuinely stricken by something bad. She knew who'd died and why, but I think she was in shock. Her eyes got a little teary, so I know she was upset.

She looked up at Verna with her brown eyes brimming with tears and full of knowledge I could never hope to have. "Verna, I raised you right. You aren't a drunk. Sure, maybe you're a hypochondriac and married to this here nerd. But you ain't a drunk like I was raised with. I ain't a drunk either because I know what that's like. Louis was. Now look at where it has gotten his sorry ass. Dead and alone."

"Why should I feel bad for someone who chose to live his life like an idiot when I learned from my daddy's mistakes and worked hard to raise two good kids?"

That quieted the room down to a hush not often heard in our house. She meant every word she'd said and she was right. My Uncle Lou didn't have much to leave behind but a legacy of funny stories about public drunkenness and very few material possessions. He didn't have a wife, kids or grandkids and had lived alone in a small house out in the country.

I felt a chill run up my spine. I hope I don't ever end up like Uncle Lou.

No sooner did the thought cross my mind did I hear a knock at the front door. My mom told my brother and I to go to our rooms and we didn't argue.

Actually, my room was probably the sanest place in the house at the moment. I gave Grandma Lucille a quick squeeze as I passed her and headed to my safe haven to get away from the mess of people that were now flooding into our house.

10 YOU CAN'T WEAR THAT!

As it turned out, Lou had a bad heart and between his chronic drinking habit and a faulty ticker, he'd had a massive heart attack and died instantly, apparently as he was making his way in our house for Sunday dinner.

His funeral was scheduled two days later and after dealing with the constant flow of people stopping by our house with food and condolences, I was exhausted already. Unfortunately, I had a visitation to attend.

We'd all had a little cry over Lou. Despite his many faults, he was a good guy with a heart of gold and would gladly lend a helping hand to those who needed it.

My tears were more over the fact that Uncle Lou died after having never really lived at all.

Grandma Lucille's speech had left an impression on me that I couldn't quite get a handle on. You always just assume that your life will work out the way it should. I mean, people grow up; they get married, have jobs, raise kids and live happily ever after all the time, right? That is how it is done.

It never occurred to me that it might not turn out that way. I could end up like Lou just as easily as anyone else.

All of this deep thought was giving me a headache.

I came out of my philosophical fog and gave myself a glance in the mirror.

My mom had gone out and gotten my outfit for Lou's viewing at the last minute. I'd ask to get out of school for the morning to go with her, but she'd insisted that I needed to go to school to 'keep things normal.'

Clearly she hadn't noticed that my generation was well known for our need to be the opposite of normal.

Since I hadn't been there to object, she'd gone hog wild and bought something that was more her tastes than mine. Even worse, she'd done it in a hurry.

The pleated navy blue skirt went a little below my knees and somehow made me look shorter than I already am. The long sleeved button up shirt was from Benetton, a store I liked, but the horizontal stripes across it were every color of the rainbow except for navy blue, so it didn't really match.

The blue patent leather Mary Janes were nice, but the pantyhose she'd gotten me were a frighteningly dark tan and made it look like I'd gotten a spray down with a bad self-tanner. Plus, I'd had to pull the hose up so high I felt paralyzed from the neck down.

"My, Lord. I look like a cracked out Punky Brewster." I said to my psychedelic reflection.

With the outfit a lost cause, I pulled my hair back in a tight ponytail, threw on some eyeliner and a little bit of lip gloss and was ready to go.

After hearing several *"MOVE ITS!"* from various places and people in the house, I hustled out to the car to meet up with the rest of the family with Grandma Lucille hot on my heels.

As I went to grab the car door handle I glanced up to see everyone staring in the direction of the sidewalk, unmoving, with their mouths hanging open. I followed their line of vision to see what had them so shocked and quickly fell into my own trance.

My Grandma Lucille was semi-jogging down the sidewalk in front of the house in a pair of purple spandex shorts, a white button up blouse and a pair of brown orthopedic shoes.

I heard my dad mumble something not at all nice and my mom just stood there looking like she might faint.

My grandma noticed our stares, stopped dead in her tracks. Looking back at all of us, she defiantly adjusted her purse strap and said, "Don't these here britches look sharp? I've got me a date with Lester Lang down to the Bingo Hall once we're done at Flanderson's."

"These pants sure do ride up, though. I'm going to need a crowbar to get out of these things."

She plopped herself down in the backseat of the car and we all piled silently in after her. After a few seconds of awkward silence, my mom put on her brave face and knew good and well she was all alone in the fight.

Talking Grandma Lucille out of something was practically impossible and none of us had any intention of trying.

Mom turned around in her seat and said, "Mother, we're going to a funeral. Are you sure you don't want to change?"

Looking genuinely confused about why my mom would consider her outfit inappropriate (even though I'm sure she knew), she held her hands up and replied, "Why? You think some dead fellah's going to get all bent out of shape over my new drawers? Probably Lou would like these here shorts. Matter of fact, those bird legs of his might have looked better in them than mine do."

My dad started to say something to that, but my mom held her hand up to stop him and turned back around in her seat. She wasn't happy and the little creases on her face said that she knew it was a useless argument.

With that, my dad started the car and the Crantz's were off to pay our respects to dearly departed Uncle Lou.

11 FUNERALS AND FLOOZIES

Flanderson's Funeral Home was in the middle of Flatwoods on the main road that ran through town. The two story brick building was designed to look more like a house than a funeral home.

The white pillars in the front that sat on each side of a porch made it look like any other porch, only fancier and more subdued, with just a few benches to sit on while you take in the fresh air.

Most of the people in our town brought their family and friends here when the good Lord called them home. Ned and Ted Flanderson, a father and son mortician team, were well respected in the community because they weren't just good at their jobs, they were genuinely nice guys.

As we walked in the front door, both of the men were waiting on us just inside the foyer and ready to greet us with outstretched hands and heartfelt condolences.

Ned, the younger Flanderson, gave my Grandma Lucille's getup a double take before helping her off with her coat.

Ted, the eldest Flanderson, was in his late 70's and probably really close to handing over the family business to his son. He had a calm demeanor and wasn't stiff like most people in his line of work. He was tall, had a head full of grey hair and was so tall he almost had to duck to get through doorways.

His wife Liana died several years back after a hard fought battle with breast cancer that she couldn't win, leaving him widowed. According to my grandma he'd become a pretty sought after commodity in the senior citizen crowd because, as she and her friends said, *'He's hot to trot and has a wallet that can really put a smile on a gal's face.'*

Will I be as weird when I get old like them? Geeze.

The inside of Flanderson's was typical. The walls were covered in deep burgundy wallpaper and the golden wall sconces were dimly lit, leaving you with a sense of calm.

Well, they were supposed to leave you with a sense of calm. I never felt calm in a funeral home and I don't think most of my family did either. Not a word was said as we all walked down the hallway towards the room where they'd put Lou and you could cut the tension with a knife.

My Uncle Lou was put in what they called the Solemn Slumber Suite. It was smaller than the other two rooms they had visitations in, but the Victorian décor made it the prettiest of the three, therefore the most requested. My Aunt Verna used to work with Ned's mom back in the day and called in a favor to get it.

Lou was all laid out in a casket made of a dark looking wood with silver handles. Someone had gotten a large flower arrangement with multi colored flowers for the top of it and there were dozens more surrounding him that had been sent from friends, family and acquaintances.

Lou himself looked like Lou, only he had that waxy sheen that I guess even pounds of makeup can't mask. He'd been put in a navy blue suit and the look on his face was peaceful.

We all looked at him for a little while, silently crying and passing around small, comforting hugs and took our moment alone with him until the people started to show up.

My Aunt Verna and I walked around and looked at the various flower arrangements and checked cards to see who sent what. It wasn't until we got to a particularly large basket sitting in the floor that we both kind of stood and stared at it blankly.

Somebody had sent a ginormous fruit basket.

In a whisper meant to keep people from overhearing, but loud enough to hurt my ears, my Aunt Verna said, "I wonder why somebody would send a fruit basket to a funeral? What are they gonna do? Shove a peach in Lou's front pocket before they close the lid? Are they just all, *"Here's a banana. My uncle Pete died awhile back and he loved bananas. Could you give him this while you're in heaven? If you don't run into him, you can eat it. I won't get mad or anything."*

I was doing my best to hold back the hysterical laughter that was threatening to escape from my throat when she added, "Sorry, I get a little nervous at viewings. I mean, there's a dead person in the room! Who doesn't get a little nervous around dead people?"

She does have a point.

I leaned down to look at the card and read it. Written in very neat cursive, it read:

Love Always,

Prudence Hannigan

"Who is this?" I said handing Aunt Verna the little card. "I've never heard of her?"

Aunt Verna took it and gave it a good hard look. "I have no idea. Maybe he had a girlfriend, but I never heard anything about it."

People started coming in and Verna placed the card back on its little plastic stick. "We will have to look into it though," Verna said. "Now I'm a little bit curious. And a whole lot nosey."

I shrugged it off and we both went over to get in the receiving line that had already started to form. An hour of hugs, kisses and handshakes passed pretty quickly, but I was ready to go home and we still had an hour left to go.

Grandma Lucille was animatedly chatting up an older lady while they both leaned over Lou's coffin to admire him. Both of them were flailing their arms around and it looked, at first, as if they were showing each other how to pedal a bicycle with their arms. But the longer they talked and moved about, the more I noticed that Grandma Lucille didn't exactly appear to be happy.

As a matter of fact, she looked downright mad.

The thought had no sooner crossed my mind when Grandma Lucille angrily stuck a finger in the woman's face and yelled, "Take that back. Take that back right now!"

Equally upset, the woman yelled, "I will not. It's true!"

"I'm telling you right now, Fiona! I ain't never had eyes for that perverted husband of yours and I don't know why you thought I was flirting with him. All I wanted to do was borrow his ink blotter to use on my Bingo card on account of mine was out!"

Without so much as a warning, Fiona stuck her finger dangerously close to Grandma Lucille's face and spit out, "You was too! You Floozy!"

The look that came over grandma's face was so scary I felt myself shrink back a little bit. She'd reached her breaking point and before Fiona knew what hit her, my grandma, who carries her purse everywhere she goes, pulled it off her shoulder and clocked her in the head.

The impact was loud enough to completely silence the chatter of the entire room.

My mom, dad and Wally started over towards the women to break it up, but it was too late. The damage had been done and we officially had a senior citizen death match on our hands.

Grandma Lucille was in full bar brawl mode and was doing her best to pummel Fiona to death with her handbag. My Uncle Wally reached them first and jumped in to try and pull them away from each other.

Unfortunately, Wally isn't a very physical kind of man and ended up being pushed back and forth between the two women like a ping pong ball. I tried to yell out a warning that he was going to get hurt, but while grandma was playing Pocketbook Ninja all over Fiona, she accidentally nailed Wally in the head and sent him hurdling backwards towards Uncle Lou's coffin.

Wally wore a hairpiece on special occasions and he'd worn it this evening. As soon as there was purse to head impact, his toupee went flying and ended up landing on dearly departed Uncle Lou's face.

That got the attention of our two elderly Fight Club members.

Breathing hard with her purse dangling in her hand, Grandma Lucille looked over at Wally and said, "For God's sakes Wally, get that rug off my brother. He looks like he's being attacked by one of them Wookie fellah's from that Star Trooper show."

Fiona added, "It's Star Wars, you idiot!"

Caught off guard yet again, Grandma Lucille's purse went flying and the first swing hit Fiona's arm with a loud crack. This time, however, she was smart enough to start backing away rather than just standing there.

As she made her way through the crowd, you could hear her yelling profanities at my grandma until, finally, the elder Flanderson got her successfully outside.

My Aunt Verna was looking just a tad bit horrified by the debacle and I'm not sure if she was more upset that her husband had been knocked around by a couple of Golden Girls or that he'd lost his hair. Whatever the case, her face was a bright red.

Chatter eventually started back up and got increasingly louder over time. My mom was over in the corner giving my grandma a lecture, my dad was sitting with my brother in a chair looking exhausted and Verna had taken Wally to the bathroom to fix his head.

As for me? I'm trying to pretend I've gone invisible. I'm hoping if I stand really still, nobody will bother me.

12 UNCLE LOU'S LEFTOVERS

Two days had passed since the viewing from hell when Uncle Lou's ashes arrived. I was creeped out just thinking about them being in our house.

They'd arrived by messenger and had been placed inside a decorative container that looked like a fatter version of a genie's bottle. The black background and red flower decoration on the outside made for a pretty urn, but the fact that there was a dead person in it kind of ruined the whole thing for me.

I was more than happy to get the scattering the ashes thing done and over with.

Uncle Lou's house was a small, one story shack out in the middle of nowhere. The light blue siding and weathered white shutters made it look almost forgotten. The front porch boards were all lying at different levels and needed some serious repair, but that wouldn't be happening now that their owner had passed.

Behind the house was a large creek that ran in both directions as far as the eye could see through the trees. It was a peaceful place and the sounds of the water made it even more so.

I understand why Lou had chosen this as his final resting place. It was beautiful and you were far enough away from roads and neighbors that all you could hear was nature.

"Okay," my mom said. "How about we do this."

We all nodded as my mom handed Grandma Lucille the urn containing Lou.

"Would you like to say something?" My mom said quietly.

My grandma turned the urn around in her hands and looked at it. My Aunt Verna and Uncle Wally were standing next to her and my mom, dad, brother and myself were standing across from her, waiting for some kind of a speech.

She started to speak, but her voice cracked on the first try so she cleared her throat and tried again. "My brother was a good man. Sure, he was an idiot sometimes and did enjoy his fair share of moonshine, but he was a good man with a good heart."

"I hope he is finally in a place where he isn't lonely and can give his mind a rest from all his troubles."

A tear escaped her eye and I walked over to stand beside her, putting my arm around her shoulders and trying to comfort her.

She looked over at me and her eyes were as wide and serious as I had ever seen them. "Millie, I want you to remember this very moment and think back to it when you feel like life isn't worth the effort or feel like giving up. Lou never lived and wasted his time here—you don't want to end up like this, alone and without much of anything to call your own. You understand me?"

I stared at her for a minute and nodded my head. "I promise."

I was shocked to find that I actually meant what I'd said. I had no intention of ever ending up so sad and lonely.

She looked over at each member of our family one by one and they all nodded back at her in agreement.

"Okay, then." She said, wiping her tears. "Let's get these suckers spread out and get out of here. I'm pretty sure I've got chiggers in my drawers by now."

I saw my dad roll his eyes, but smile despite himself.

We all gathered in a line beside the creek and held hands as grandma lifted the lid on the urn. She heaved it back, let the contents fly and the little specs of Lou hit the water and were washed away with the current.

As she tossed the ashes, she said one last thing. "Oh, Louis, how sad we are to see you go. But, we leave you with the words of the very classy George Burns- *'I'm very pleased to be here. Let's face it; at my age I'm pleased to be anywhere.' Amen."*

We should let grandma do all of our funerals. You can at least die knowing they'd be entertaining.

She continued to scatter, but it seemed like there was an awfully lot of Lou in that one small container. It was also a little strange that every time she heaved, a loud clank would follow. It reminded me of someone banging on a glass with a fork.

"What is that noise?" my brother asked.

That was followed by several questions from all of us and possible suggestions about what it was.

"Is that the lid?"

"Don't sling it so hard, you'll break it!"

"Shake it harder!"

"Ewe! I think the wind blew ashes on my shoes!"

"I think it got in my mouth!"

We all looked over at grandma and she looked as perplexed as we all were. She gave the urn a shake and the harder she did it, the louder the noise got until she got fed up and just turned it upside down.

What was left of Lou floated out and into the water, but whatever was causing the noise was still inside. In her frustration, she finally just started banging on the bottom like you would if you were trying to get the last of the ketchup out of the bottle.

That's when it came out, landing in the creek with a splash.

We all crouched around the unexplained shiny object, which was now lying in the water on the edge of the creek bed.

"What is that thing?" My mom asked in awe.

"Why hell, I don't know Earnestine. Somebody get down there and pick it up!" grandma replied, looking sincerely baffled.

We all spent a few minutes arguing over who was going to touch it when my dad finally stepped up to the task. God bless his bravery because goodness knows I have no desire to touch anything that once touched a dead dude-even if he was family.

Holding it up to the light you could see that it was a shiny round object and made of a very lightweight, silver metal that looked to be kind of expensive. We all spent a few minutes staring at it, trying to figure out what it was.

"Oh my good Lord in Heaven!" My Aunt Verna squealed. "I know what that is!"

Once she was done clutching her chest and hyperventilating, she was finally able to tell us what we were looking at. "That is Lou's hip replacement!"

I don't think I've ever seen my dad move so fast. He dropped the hip and back peddled away. Actually, we all backed away and just kind of stood there in shock.

"I'll be damned." My Grandma Lucille said. "You reckon I could take that home and save it in case I need one? It'd save me a fortune."

Cries of disgust echoed through the woods and it took us a minute or two to convince grandma that you couldn't reuse a hip replacement.

After that, we all went and piled back into the car and headed home.

Uncle Lou's life may have been uneventful, but his death had been anything but. That doesn't make up for what he'd lost, though. I wonder if you carry your regrets with you when you die, or do they just float away when your heart stops beating?

For Lou's sake, I hope it's the latter.

13 RETURN OF THE FAIRY RUDEMOTHER

"Wake up, little lady! No time to sleep!"

I was hearing it, but afraid to open my eyes because I wasn't sure if I was dreaming again or not.

The feel of the dirt beneath my cheek was a good indication that I wasn't, but just to be sure I kept my eyes closed and tried to mentally prepare myself for what I was about to face.

The person speaking was becoming more aggravated by the second and her tone was getting a little sharper with every word. "You are a pain in my ass, you know? I have better things I could be doing!"

Clearly tired of my possum act, I felt a foot nudge the back of my head in an effort to get me up.

I cracked an eyelid open and from the corner of my eye I saw her. She was still wearing the same clothes, carrying the same purse and still had on the little black hat, but her face wasn't nearly as serene as I remembered.

Actually, she looked kind of ticked off.

I rolled over on my back and could feel that there was a combination of flower petals and dirt stuck to the side of my face, but at this point I am beyond caring about my appearance. I opened my eyes all the way and there she stood in all her glory.

The Fairy Rudemother from hell.

"Who are you?" I asked, sounding a little more crazed than I intended. "What in the name of all that is Holy is going on here?"

She put her hand down in an effort to help me up and I accepted. My joints were stiff from my freak out and the nap on the ground that followed it. I felt like I had a serious hangover.

For the third time now, I started to brush the crap off of me, starting this time with my hair. I reached up and heard the dirt fall as I gave it a shake. Making my way down the rest of me, I did my best to sweep off the excess and quickly realized that it was a losing battle.

"It's not going to help, Millie. Give it a rest. You're a mess." The little old lady without manners rudely said.

"Thanks. I appreciate the support and good cheer. Now, who the heck are you, why am I here and what in the hell is the deal with the cemetery?" I asked, officially out of patience. "Are you real?"

I reached forward and gave her a light tap on the shoulder and wasn't surprised when I made contact. She swayed a little bit and smiled knowingly.

"Millie, this isn't a movie, you dummy. You think I'm made of air? A ghost?" She then started waving her hands all over the place and moaning. To drive the point home, she did more moaning and topped that off with a poorly hummed rendition of the theme song to the Twilight Zone.

"Okay!" I said throwing my hands in the hair. "Knock that off! There's no need to be a smarty pants about it. How can you blame me for assuming you're not real? It isn't like people end up in my situation all the time!"

She immediately stopped and as if a switch had been flipped, a serious look crawled across her face. "Okay, you ready to listen now?"

"Yes."

"Good. Okay, where to start?" she looked around us as if she was missing something and said, "Well, I'd ask you to sit down but I have no intention of sitting in this filth, so you're going to have to either be calm, or faint in a soft spot."

"Anyways," she said. "I just want to tell you you're going about this all wrong. Believe it or not, you should feel lucky to be here."

"Doing what wrong? Wrong attitude? How is that even possible? Is there a right way to be?" I asked, confused.

"This! And yes!" she replied, stretching her arms out in front of her.

I looked down at her arms and waited for something to appear. Like a miracle or even a moist towelette to clean myself off with.

Nothing did.

"What the hell are you doing?" she asked, letting her arms go back down to her sides.

"Well, I don't actually know. Waiting on a miracle I guess?"

"My good God, Millie. You have got to be the dumbest smart kid I know."

"What did you just say?" I asked her, staring as hard at her face as I could in the hope of recognizing it. I knew that phrase and had sadly heard it more than once in my life.

She looked back at me as if she'd realized her mistake, but repeated herself anyways. "You have got to be the dumbest smart kid I know."

She smiled a little at that and kept going. "Give it up. You're not meant to know some things in this world and who I am is one of them. So, right now, let's just get past that mystery and move on to the more important ones. Okay?"

I nodded my head, but kept her small slip up filed away for later. It was like remembering the lyrics to a song but not being able to think of the actual title and it was driving me insane.

"Okay, then," she said seriously. "You listening?"

"Well, I don't know. There are an awfully lot of distractions around here what with all the dead people to talk to. I'm not sure if I can focus." I looked at her with what I hoped was my best sarcastic face. "Duh."

"Smartass!"

"Rude and creepy!"

"I may be old, but I can still kick you little rear end from here to Tuesday. Either shut it or figure it out on your own!"

I bit my tongue. I needed her, even if I didn't much like her at the moment. I gave her a small nod of the head to continue.

"Now, then. As I was saying." She said, holding her arms back up. "You're going about it all wrong."

I waited on her to continue, afraid if I said something like--*You already said that*--it would come out unmannerly and make her disappear again.

She pointed down at the grave I'd just woken up on top of (which was totally gross and gave me the chills) and said, "It's possible you don't know this person as well as you may think you do."

"I'm not sure of anything at all." I said. "I don't know if I feel sad because somebody died, or I've lost somebody I love, or lost my marbles or what? Can you be a little more specific? Like how about giving me a name? Initials? Something it rhymes with, even?"

For the second time since I'd first made eye contact with her during the funeral, she appeared genuinely sad and behind all the sass I could tell that whoever she was, she and I were connected in a way that went much deeper than I'd originally thought.

"Millie, honey," she said with a whisper. "The person in the ground beneath our feet isn't as important as why you're here, where you are, right now."

I looked at her and felt my eyebrow cock. "And this is something you felt like you should appear out of the mist to tell me that I didn't already know?"

"After your whole hissy fit with the flowers, I felt like you might need a little reminder. And, by the way, what a mess you made."

With a cock of her own eyebrow and another one of those annoying smirks, she added, "I suppose now you'll just have live in it, huh?"

I looked back down at the various petals and stems that I'd torn to shreds and felt the scratches on my arms sting a little as a reminder of my outburst. "Pretty tacky of me, I guess. But you'd be mad, too." I said shamefully. "I didn't know I'd done as much damage as I had."

I felt a hand land on my shoulder that was gone as quick as it got there and knew this was her attempt to comfort me.

Before I even looked up I knew that I was, yet again, alone.

"Well, crap!" I yelled. The noise echoed off the marble walls of a nearby mausoleum and I winced.

What time is it? How long have I been here now? I have no idea and possibly no hope of ever knowing anything ever again if I don't figure this out.

What if I get stuck here forever? Is this hell? Am I doomed to spend the rest of eternity being driven insane by Granny Know-It-All?

Maybe I'm dreaming?

Whatever it is, it sucks. Big time.

I did know one thing-I was sick of looking at the same old grave and needed some new scenery.

14 PENNY FOR YOUR THOUGHTS

You know how sometimes, you start out thinking one thing and ten minutes later your train of thought has dragged you so far away from the original topic that you have no clue how you got there?

That's where I am right now. I've been wandering around the cemetery grounds trying to work this whole thing out in my head, but I don't seem to be making any progress.

I've always been scatterbrained, but this is ridiculous.

I'd made my way to a large angel sculpture that had been here ever since I can remember. It was so big you could see it from the road and because it sat just a little ways down from both the middle and high schools I went to as a kid, I always made a conscious effort to look at it as we passed each morning.

I don't know why, but it was almost a ritual for me. Every time my dad drove me to school, and even when I started to drive myself, I would crane my neck just to get a glimpse of her.

She was a lot bigger up close. Her stony eyes were cast towards the ground in sorrow and prayer, but the expression on her face was serene. Her wings were stretched out to her sides as far as they would go and looked to be holding all of those buried here in their embrace.

It was if that was her job-to protect everyone inside these hallowed grounds and the loved ones who came to visit them. Even though her head was bowed, her face said that she did it because she knew, without a shadow of a doubt, that everything would be okay.

Well, it's nice to know somebody around here has it all figured out.

It was very comforting and looking at her calmed my mind. I suppose I felt this way when I saw her as a kid; I just never stopped long enough to really think about it.

I walked over and propped myself up on the base at her feet, exhausted. As I looked around, I noticed that some of the graves were overflowing with flowers and small trinkets left by family and friends. But a lot of the others looked as if they hadn't been visited since the day they were put there.

I remembered my Uncle Lou and it made me sad to think that there were so many people out there with nobody. At least Lou had us.

Did these people have family at all? Wives? Husbands? Daughters? Sons? Moms and dads?

Were they genuinely bad people who nobody wanted to get near or were they like Lou and just decided to give up before they really gave living a chance at all?

Sure, there have been a few people who have ventured into my world and gone out of it just as quick as they came in. But, in all fairness, that is a universally accepted truth.

Life would be boring if it wasn't peppered with new faces from time to time.

It's the people who stay that mean the most. They are what you count on when you start to feel cracks forming in your foundation.

Maybe my Uncle Lou was just tired of all the in and out and just stuck with what he knew?

After the funeral, my Aunt Verna did some detective work on the mysterious Prudence and her fruit basket. She found out from Prudence herself that she and Lou had been in love back when they were teenagers, but Lou flew off the rails around that time and started drinking.

She'd told my Aunt Verna that she loved the man she knew, but hated the man he'd become.

While that didn't explain the why behind the fruit basket (Aunt Verna said she was probably just an odd lady to begin with), it certainly explained a lot about Lou himself.

Unfortunately, she'd had to give him up and that was Lou's final breaking point. He knew he'd turned himself into a monster, but even though he loved her, he'd never tried to better himself.

It's like he just sat down and never got back up again. He didn't care anymore and, when he died, it showed.

It was that very thought that made me sit up and take notice that, aside from a couple of obscure conversations with Granny Grumps, I was actually alone right now.

Very alone.

15 MY GENERATION

They call us Generation X.

I'm not really sure why, exactly, but I don't much care either. I'm a child of the 90's and proud of it.

I have a closet full of flannels and band t-shirts, a CD collection full of depressing grunge rock (and some R&B that I am frequently teased about), I could take out stock in Converse tennis shoes, purposely fray the end of every pair of jeans I own and would do a soap opera star proud with my ability to sit around listening to love songs while having in-head musical montages about whatever boy I happen to be obsessing over at the time.

Asserting your individualism isn't something new to teenagers, but my generation somehow managed to take it to a level that is both bizarre and inspiring all at the same time.

Vernon High School held grades 9-12. Each of us fell into a category based on our social, musical and fashion preferences.

There are Skaters, Goths, Stoners, Jocks, Skanks, Nerds, Neo Hippies, Freaks, Geeks, Feminists, Metal Heads, Grunge, Lush's, Players and, unfortunately, some straight up idiots.

We're also a fertile bunch. Our generation has helped usher in an entirely new set of standards where teen pregnancy is concerned.

The school building itself has been here so long that I think even my dad graduated from this very same building back in the 60's. The school colors, maroon and gold respectively, made up the general paint scheme of the entire inside. The hallways were always lined with various signs about clubs, football games and the usual array of Say No to Drugs posters.

I was sad to note that today they were mostly about the upcoming Homecoming Formal, for which I had no date to speak of.

Not that I'd gone out of my way to find one, really. I was a notoriously bad flirter and always ended up embarrassing someone when I tried. That someone was usually me.

The dance is on Friday and today is Wednesday. Unless a miracle happens, I probably won't be going.

As I walked down the hallways towards my locker, all I heard was talk of dresses and who was going with whom. Maybe I'm bitter, maybe I'm jealous, whatever the case-I wish they'd all just shoosh about it already.

I saw Maggie a little ways down the hallway waiting on me, all leaned up against the metal row of lockers looking smug.

"Word up, Crantz!" she yelled down the hallway.

"Why are you so cheery this early in the morning?" I spit out at her. "And seriously with that shirt? Hanging out with you is bad for my eyesight."

"Wow. Good mood today, huh? Well, get over it. I have good news."

I stopped stacking my books and looked at her, already knowing what she was about to tell me. "What is it? Or should I say who is it?"

She squealed and jumped around in a circle before she finally got around to spitting it out. "Lenny Vance asked me to the dance!"

She squealed again and I couldn't help but laugh. Her happy dance kind of looked like she was doing The Erkel.

"Awesome." I said, hoping I sounded excited for her and not green with envy like I actually was.

She grabbed my shoulder. "Wait! That isn't all!"

Uh oh. I stopped putting my books in my locker and turned around to give her the stink eye. "What did you do?

"Don't be mad at me, okay? It isn't like I've arranged to give away your hand in marriage or anything. It's just a dance and I don't want to go by myself."

I tried not to roll my eyes, but couldn't keep my foot from tapping the floor impatiently. "Who?"

"Chucky Peabody"

My mouth fell open. Chucky Peabody was about the grossest kid I'd ever met. He was short, loud and had a really bad case of acne that he would openly pick at in our English class.

"No! No, no, no! No way. That kid is scary!"

She didn't look nearly as ashamed of herself as she should and I knew she probably wasn't. "Just, please!" she yelled. "Do it for me? I mooned Freddie Gritz for you that time! I would do it for you!"

"Oh, you would not!" I said dramatically. "I don't know if you recall, but you once said that even if Chucky wasn't gross, you could never date a guy named Chucky because it made you think of the pizza place with the all of the animatronic animals."

"I did not!"

"You did."

"Please!"

I bit my lip and thought about it. I wouldn't mind getting all dressed up for a change. And I DID want to go to the dance.

But Chucky Peabody?

"Fine. I'll go. But you listen here, asshat. You owe me one for this."

"Fine by me!" she replied in a sing songy voice. She was still jumping around as we walked down the hallway to first period.

Just as we'd almost made it, Chucky and Lenny walked past us and Maggie excitedly shared the news that we would accept their offer.

Chucky smiled a greasy smile and no matter how hard I prayed that he wouldn't come near me, he did- and he kept right on coming. The closer he got, the more I pressed myself against the lockers behind me.

I was trapped and he knew it. He put his hand above my head and invaded my comfort zone so much I could barely breathe. I was afraid to move.

"So," he said, twitching his eyebrows up and down. "You and me, babe. You and me."

His last you and me was punctuated with his finger pointing creepily back and forth between us. I was tempted to slap it out of my face, but decided against it at the last minute.

"Millie Crantz, you are a foxy lady and you will be flattered to know I've had my eye on your for a while now."

I was not flattered. At all. Chucky, however, ignored the horrified look on my face and continued.

"You are a princess and I shall be your prince. I'll pick you up at 7:00 on Friday for a little dinner, a little dancing and a whole lot of Chucky lovin'."

With that, he backed off and he and Lenny went to their own class, but not before he looked back at us and blew me a kiss.

I shuddered from my head to my toes, and not with pleasure. I gave Maggie an extremely dirty look and hoped she knew exactly how much I hated her at the moment.

"Hey, don't be giving me dirty looks. He did say you were a foxy princess, so that's pretty awesome, right?" Her statement was broken up by some extremely annoying giggles that I didn't appreciate.

"You-suck."

"Whatever, Princess Foxy. We're going to be late. Let's go do some learnin'."

Walking into class I could already feel the dread of the dance sinking through my pores.

Chucky Freaking Peabody. Yuck.

16 SHOPPING WITH THE FAMILY

The Homecoming Dance was formal, so I had to go shopping. I would rather have gone with friends, but unless they'd won the lottery at some point, my mom was my only choice.

Since this was technically my first formal, all the women in my family were excited and decided they needed to go with us to pick out my dress. I'd begged my mom not to allow it and even offered to clean house if she told them to stay home.

She was offended that I would even consider not taking them with us.

"Millicent May Crantz! That is your family you're talking about! They are excited for you. You shouldn't keep them away!"

"Mom," I replied as level headed as I could. "Grandma Lucille wears those crazy shirts! Did you see the one she has on today? It has an elephant picture on the front and the trunk of it runs down the right sleeve! I don't think she's really the fashion maven type."

I continued on to make my point.

"And, seriously. Aunt Verna dresses like, well, you've seen it. She likes gold stuff and animal prints that make you dizzy when you look at them too long."

"Forget it, Millie. They're going."

I gave up. It was a lost cause. I was going shopping with a semi-senile granny, a hypochondriac who fancies zebra prints and my mom. Fan-tastic.

All four of us piled in the car and off we went.

Grandma Lucille had taken shotgun, my mom was driving and Aunt Verna and I got the backseat.

While my mom and grandma had their own hushed conversation, Verna decided we should have one as well.

"I can't believe you're old enough to go to a dance, Millie. It seems like it was just yesterday you were running around the house with a pile in your diaper." She'd said that last sentence with such an air of sentimentality, I had to smile. She'd meant it to be nice, but sadly she always sounds off color like that.

"Yep," I said with a smile. "No more piles in my diapers. I can go potty all by myself now."

"Smarty pants."

We both chuckled and I turned my attention back to the window.

"Speaking of using the bathroom…."

Verna went on to explain to me that since she and Wally had gotten married, she'd become suddenly paranoid about the odor that comes from a number two and worries that Wally will smell it.

I spent a lot of the time she was explaining it to me alternating between rolling my eyes, laughing hysterically and being kind of grossed out.

"I can't do it." She said throwing her hands up in the air. Her hair was stacked so high on her head today that the top was pressing against the roof of the car. "It is impossible for me to concentrate. If you had any idea how hard it is, you wouldn't be doing all that eye rolling you're doing."

"Well, that's just crazy. I can do it just about anywhere! Well, except for in those portable toilets that have the blue stuff in them. Those things are gross. Why do you need to concentrate anyways? You're not doing nuclear physics or anything."

"Why am I even discussing this with you? You're a child. Children don't worry about this stuff like adults do."

My Aunt Verna has always been strange, but this just takes the cake. I've never heard of a grown woman taking issue with doing a number two in her own house. I mean, she married Wally about two years ago. You'd think she'd have gotten used to it by now.

I had no real interest in listening to Verna drone on about their new life together, only because I was busy worrying about all of the other crap in my life.

But Verna, in a sense, also had a lot of crap on her mind. I couldn't escape the conversation, so I figured I may as well participate and did my best to pay attention.

"Wally has a sensitive nose. If I just run in there and let it rip, he'll know. He'll smell it! Or, God forbid, he'll hear me doing it." She accentuated that last sentence with a dramatic shiver to demonstrate how appalling it would be if Wally were to hear her poop.

"Then," she continued on. "He'll have this image in his head of me pooping. Before you know it, we'll both get brave and start leaving the door wide open. Eventually we'll be discussing the weather; him in the shower and me on the toilet. I wouldn't be able to look him in the eye ever again. I don't care how much you love them, a person's pooping habits and rituals should remain a private practice. Don't you agree?"

That was something I think we could both agree on. "Does Wally poop at your house?"

"Of course he does! My house stinks to high heaven every time the man so much as steps foot in that bathroom. I think he has colon issues, personally, but that is neither here nor there."

She stopped and thought for a minute before continuing on.

"This has become a serious issue. I drive the thirteen miles between our house and yours just to use the restroom. What do you suppose would happen if I got food poisoning or some sort of viral thing? You can't drive all that way with a bad stomach. You also have to consider that it won't always be as pretty outside as it is today. What if there's snow, or traffic, or I hit a dog? What if I have a car accident and they cut me out of the car to find that I've quite literally had the crap scared out of me? "

For some reason, I actually stopped to think about the answer to that question.

"Probably you'd be spending a lot of time at the car wash because you couldn't make it in time. Or, maybe you'll just need a whole new car."

"You're right." Verna said thoughtfully. "I'm going to have to figure this out. I can't afford a new car. Hell, I can't even afford to go to the car wash that often."

After that, we both went back to our window watching and stayed quiet the rest of the trip. I felt my stomach start doing flip flops when we pulled into the parking lot. I hope this isn't as awful as I imagine it will be.

We all got out of the car and looked up at the sign on the front. The giant neon pink letters scrawled on the front of the store said Foxy Lady.

The irony of the only formal dress store in town and my date's compliment was not lost on me.

I was considering pulling off a fake fainting attack but heard the bell from the store's door ring and realized everyone else was already going in.

I unhappily followed them, but only because I know if I turn up missing my mom will have a conniption fit and send the National Guard after me.

The inside wasn't fancy and the walls were old plywood that had clearly been put there sometime in 1970 and not moved since. The racks of dresses scattered all over the floor were practically overflowing with poofs, lace and sparkles.

We all made a beeline for our own racks and started digging. With squeals of delight and tons of *"Oh My, Millie, you'd look goooorrrggeouuus in this!"* I told each member of the family they could choose one dress for me to try one. If I don't set limits, we'll be here until I need to start shopping for my wedding dress.

The dressing room was the size of a cupboard and the owner, a woman named Luanne Friskel who was missing one of her front teeth, made you put a pair of pantyhose over your head to make sure none of your makeup rubbed off on the dress you were trying on.

How insane is that? I looked like a bank robber trying on fancy dresses. I asked her three times if she was sure whether or not they'd been used and she assured me they hadn't.

The dress I'd chosen was black and simple. The material was a kind of velvet and the top of it came down off my shoulders in a respectable way. As I put it on, I was a little thrown off by how much cleavage a girl needed to pull it off, so I discarded that one without even leaving the dressing room.

The next one was my Aunt Verna's choice and I almost laughed when I pulled it out of the plastic. It was mermaid cut and had a slit up the side that was so high I was afraid I might expose my hoo-ha if I walked a certain way. The blue sequins that practically covered the entire dress gave it an 80's vibe that I wasn't comfortable with, but I walked out to show it off, anyways.

"Oh, my! I love it!" My Aunt Verna squealed. "Gorgeous!"

My mom looked at me sideways and did a little walk around it while frowning. "This dress is the biggest mess I've ever seen!"

Grandma Lucille was just laughing. She was laughing so hard she was bent over in the floor holding her stomach.

I smiled at her and did a little curtsey. "Is that a no, grandma?"

Still laughing, she stood up and looked at me. "Millie honey, that is a hell no! You look like one of them Vegas showgirls."

I took that as my cue to run back in my dressing room for the next dress.

My mom's choice was more like mine, only a lot more colorful. It was princess cut with multicolored sequin polka dots sewn all over a black satin background.

"No way, mom!" I yelled outside to the waiting women. "This thing looks like something from a Sonny and Cher Special. Or a game of Twister."

I got no reply to that, but I imagine she was frantically looking for something else to torture me with. I hurried on with grandma's choice so I could get out there and stop the madness before it started.

Grandma Lucille's choice was a deep navy blue satin number with a square cut neckline. At first it looked old fashioned, but when I put it on I noticed that it fit me just right from head to toe. It didn't have any lace or giant slits up the side. It was very mid-40's and I loved it.

Simple and classy.

I shoved open the dressing room door with a flourish and paraded around in front of the dressing mirror with pride. I was a little shocked nobody was saying anything and started to feel a little like an idiot. I turned around to give my butt a quick glance over my shoulder and saw them all gazing at me slack jawed.

That's when they all started to cry. And when I say cry, I'm talking full on boo-hooing. I just stood on the little dress platform and tried to quietly tell them all to shut up.

Once they'd dried themselves up and gave me the okay signal, which was basically just a bunch of sobby incoherent speech, I went back in to the dressing room and morphed back into plain old Millie again.

Before we left, we bought jewelry and shoes to match. The shoes we'd chosen were extremely high in the heel department and I was worried about getting around in them without breaking my face off. I made a mental note to practice walking in them a few times before the dance rolled around, otherwise I'd end up at the hospital.

Grandma Lucille somehow managed to wander over into the underwear section and after practically screaming, "Come over here and look at these here underpants, Millie. You need some of these?" I had to go over and stay with her to keep her from embarrassing the crap out of me.

Once I'd gotten over to her, she spent most of that time trying to talk me into buying a thong.

"Millie, men like women that wear pretty underpants." She said with the voice of a preacher. "You go on and buy yourself some of them thongs they wear these days. I got me some of them glittery ones that have cherry pictures on em'." She said patting her behind. "That's how I landed Bernard Stuben before he up and died on me. That Bernard sure did love my glittery drawers." She paused after that and looked upwards as if remembering something.

"Only problem is they aren't real comfy on account of that string that goes up your butt."

Just as I thought it couldn't get worse, she bent over to pick up a bra out of the floor that she'd knocked off a rack. I was shocked to find that her thong days had not ended with Mr. Stuben's passing. She was wearing a pair today.

"You all ready to go?" my mom asked walking over with our purchases.

"Yes!" I yelled louder than I intended. "Please, Dear Lord, yes."

After learning your grandmother wears thongs, going to a dance with Chucky Peabody doesn't sound so bad.

It's still pretty bad, though.

17 A FAMILY AFFAIR

It was finally Friday afternoon and Prince Peabody was supposed to be here any minute.

I was, as usual, not ready and running behind.

My mom had insisted that someone else do my hair and makeup because she said she "Couldn't have me running around in an expensive dress looking like an Amazon woman."

The woman who fixed my hair had given it just a few loose curls and pulled the front back on each side of my head. She threw in a sparkly barrette my mom had run out and gotten at the last minute and I have to say, it doesn't look half bad.

The makeup was another story. I'd gone to the makeup counter at a department store and the lady had painted my face up like a hair band groupie. When she first gave me a mirror to look, I screamed a little bit.

The first thing I did we got home was run to the bathroom and wash it all off. I reapplied it my way only a little more glamorous to suit the occasion.

I was sliding my feet into my shoes when the doorbell rang. I knew Chucky had come in when I heard my mom say, "Oh! Cute as a button, aren't you!"

Yeah, he was cute alright. Not.

I walked out of my room and tried to remember to breathe as I made my way out to the front door. The entire family, including my grandmother and Verna, were fawning over Chucky's tie and hair when they all turned to look at me.

My dad's face was priceless and, like any good dad who is proud of his daughter and thinks she's the most beautiful thing ever, he lit up a little bit when he saw me.

I smiled at him and he nodded back. That was the nice thing about our relationship. It was easy and honest.

My brother was looking at me as if I'd just walked off the Starship Enterprise, which was not a big surprise. My mom gave him a nudge and he said, "You don't look ugly."

"Thanks, butt face." I replied with a smarmy grin. I knew my mom had made him say it, but I didn't care. I'll take what I can get.

My mom, grandmother and Verna were all crying and between the three of them, they were having trouble speaking coherently. My mom managed to get out the word "Pictures!"

Chucky actually looked presentable today. He was wearing a black suit, a black tie and his short blonde hair actually looked like he'd run a brush through it for a change.

He held up a clear plastic container with a little corsage in it. The corsage itself consisted of two small, white roses attached to a navy blue arm band. It had been garnished with some kind of glittery silver things and was actually quite pretty.

So far so good.

My mom had us get our picture made in every room of the house, I think. If I had to pretend to be pinning his boutonniere on one more time, I might go insane.

"Okay!" I yelled. "We should go. We're meeting Maggie and Lenny at O'Hare's Steakery and if we don't get going now, we'll be late."

Twelve pictures later, we'd made our way back to the front door.

Looking as tall and stern as I'd ever seen him, my dad leaned over and gave Chucky a rundown of the rules for dating his teenage daughter.

"Back here right after the dance. No questions asked. It ends at eleven and I want her back here at five after. You go to dinner, the dance and then home. That's it. She comes back with even a scratch, dead meat."

His eyes were like saucers as he looked back at my dad. "Yes, sir. No problem, sir."

My dad nodded and backed away. I'm not sure, but I could swear I saw him smile a little.

My mom repeated my dad's rules, in much more pleasant phrasing, and gave Chucky's hand a quick shake before grabbing me up in a bear hug. As she was pulling away she whispered, "Please, for the love of God, be a lady this evening. Don't get into trouble."

"Have faith, mom." I said back, smiling broadly.

I was ready to walk out the door, but because they'd been so uncharacteristically quiet, I forgot my grandma and Aunt Verna were even there. I was impressed when Chucky made the effort to shake their hands and say goodbye before we left.

Verna behaved herself and just smiled. Grandma Lucille, however, is incapable of behaving and decided that she'd give Chucky a little advice of her own.

"It's raining outside, so you all be careful. Millie ain't so great at walking in them new heels of hers and might fall down, so I expect you to pick her up if need be."

I felt my face turn bright red and Chucky giggled because I think he thought she was joking, but she wasn't. I'd been trying to figure these heels out since we'd gotten them home and I had the bruises on my butt to prove that I hadn't quite gotten the hang of it yet.

I tried pulling Chucky away and out the door, but grandma still had a firm grip on his hand.

"Also, you should probably know that Millie here once had a phobia of windshield wipers. Why, her mom would turn those things on and she'd about crap her pants. I only tell you this on account of it's raining outside and if she starts freaking out you should be prepared. She hasn't done it for a lot of years now. But, better safe than sorry, I say. "

Nobody spoke after that wonderful revelation and the uncomfortable silence was making me even antsier than I already was.

"Anyways," she said releasing his hand. "It was nice to meet you. You two better run along. Have a good time and be safe."

I grabbed hold of Chucky's suit jacket and practically yanked him out the door. We were walking to the car when I heard his giggles cut through the sound of the rain.

"What? What's so damn funny?" I asked sharply.

"Dude, you were really afraid of windshield wipers?"

"Shut-up! And, no! She's just old and stuff. She gets confused."

That was partly true. She was old and did sometimes get confused. Sadly, I really had been terrified of windshield wipers as a kid. I just didn't want the world to know it.

He opened my door for me and I threw myself down in the seat. As soon as my head was all the way in the car I was enveloped in an invisible cloud of men's cologne. My nose felt like somebody had shoved matchsticks up in them.

As he got in the driver's seat, I looked at him to see if he was suffocating too. He didn't seem to notice, so I didn't say anything.

Besides, I was impressed that he'd been so polite to my family and did the whole car door thing, so I figured I'd cut him a break for a change.

Then, as if he'd switched personalities completely, he turned, did the creepy eyebrow thing again and said, "You look so good I could cover you in barbeque sauce and work you like a rib!"

There are very few things that can stun me into absolute silence and this one tripped me up enough that I had to think about it for a minute.

I swallowed the bile that was threatening to come up my throat and smiled as nicely as I could. "Say something like that again and you're going to find yourself out in my yard with one of my mom's garden gnomes up your ass."

He nodded slightly and looked genuinely shocked at my reply. "Duly noted." He said seriously. "No barbeque sauce."

I thought my threat would be enough to put a stopper in his mouth, but I was wrong.

"What about Ranch Dressing? Or Jell-O? You like Jell-O?"

I was going to kill Maggie when I got my hands on her.

18 JUST SAY NO

We met Maggie and Lenny at O'Hare's Steakery, one of the better restaurants in town. We considered it fancy because it was the only place in town that didn't have a buffet or menu items with a Mc in front of them.

Maggie's dress was black, low-cut and not like anything I'd ever seen her in. Her long blonde hair had been straightened and hung down her back gracefully. And, for the first time since I'd known her, she'd put on makeup.

She looked absolutely beautiful and she seemed quite smitten with her date. While I was happy that she was happy, part of me still wanted to beat the crap out of her for setting me up with Chucky.

I can't complain too much. Chucky had behaved himself fairly well during dinner, but I owe most of that to Lenny for keeping him occupied. I think he knew I wasn't comfortable and went out of his way to make sure Chucky stayed out of my hair.

Lenny was actually good looking guy. His dark hair was just long enough that it reached his eyebrows and it was parted in the middle to keep it out of his pretty blue eyes. He was wearing a dark blue suit and his tie had a picture of Bevis and Butthead on the front.

If all that didn't make him cute enough, he played the guitar, too.

I am embarrassed to say that I spent more time looking at Maggie's date than I did my own.

The car ride to the high school seemed like it last forever because we all took Lenny's car and I got stuck sitting in the back with Prince Chucky.

The parking lot was already jam packed, so I we had to hoof it a bit through the grass to get to the gym. Me and my heels just barely made it in one piece and I'd bet my left ankle would be swollen in the morning.

As we walked in, Alphaville's Forever Young was blaring, bouncing off the walls of the gym and flying right back in your face. Most of the couples were slow dancing and looked genuinely happy. Some of them were standing about thirty feet away from each other looking all freaked out, but there were several others doing the exact opposite and just straight up getting freaky.

The theme to the dance was the intentionally campy Under the Sea. Whoever was in charge of decorations had gone all out on the cornball and there were pictures of poorly painted cardboard fish, blue streamers and fake plastic trees scattered around the gym. They'd even found gigantic clear beach balls and the people on the dance floor were batting it around willy nilly to keep it in the air.

"Bubbles!" Maggie yelled, running into the fray with Lenny on her heels.

I looked over to find Chucky standing dangerously close to me and scooted over a little. He was fidgeting and it seemed like he might be talking to himself, but I couldn't hear what he was saying over the music.

Abruptly he turned, held out his hand and screamed, "Do you want to dance?"

He still had his hand held out and I have to admit, being the only couple not dancing was pretty crappy. I decided to just give up the good fight and go out for a dance.

"Just one." I said seriously.

I grabbed his hand and he led me over to the edge of the dance floor. I was surprised at how tentative he was when he put his hands on my hips.

Relieved he wasn't going to be a weirdo about it, I put my hands on his shoulders and we started to sway.

I don't think we'd been going for more than thirty seconds when the song ended and Blind Melon's No Rain came in quickly to replace it.

We were headed to the concession stand (that two seconds of wobbling back and forth was exhausting) and Lenny and Maggie intercepted us at the door.

Maggie's face was flushed and so was Lenny's, and I smiled at the two of them despite myself. They were holding hands and by all appearances, I would bet their dance had gone really well.

"Having fun?" Maggie asked with a twinkle in her eye.

"Not as much fun as SOME people." I replied, cocking an eyebrow at her.

She looked at Lenny and they both giggled a little before turning their attentions back to Chucky and I.

"You want to get out of here?" Lenny asked. He reached in his suit coat's secret pocket and pulled out a green flask that was so big I wondered how nobody had noticed a lump.

I froze in place and couldn't help but picture an egg being cracked into a frying pan and hearing a man with a deep voice say, "THIS is your brain on drugs."

I chuckled a little at myself and looked over at Maggie who was looking everywhere but at me. Chucky and Lenny were both staring holes in my head, waiting on an answer.

And this is where I screw up in life-decision making. I only had two answers to choose from here and I knew which one I SHOULD choose, but that didn't stop me from picking the wrong one, anyways.

"Fine." I said seriously. "But if you're drinking, I'm driving. I'd rather not wake up dead tomorrow."

"Deal!" Lenny quickly spat out.

He tossed me his car keys and we left.

19 HAPPY MOUNTAIN HIGH

We ended up driving up to a place called Happy Mountain which was about a 15 minute drive from school. I know where the happy part came from, but it wasn't really a mountain at all. It was a small clearing that sat at the top of a hill out in BFE where people came to make out and do other non-ladylike things.

I'd been up here a few times, but always during the day and it was usually to pick blackberries with Grandma Lucille. There were no lights, so it was dark enough that you could barely see your hand in front of your face.

I left the car's headlights on and we all got out. Maggie and I sat on the roof of the car and she took several small sips from Lenny's flask while I did my best to give her 'quit it' looks out of the corner of my eye.

After about an hour of prodding and teasing by everyone, I quit fighting it and gave in to my curiosity. I tipped the flask up and the cheap whiskey filled my mouth to almost overflowing and I dribbled a little down the front of my dress.

My concern about my clothes quickly disappeared when I realized that I was having a little trouble swallowing it. It was so strong my throat caved in on itself and I gagged, sputtered and moaned until I finally swallowed what I hadn't been able to spit out.

Embarrassed, I tried again. I hadn't gotten down much of my first drink, so one more wasn't going to do anything.

The second one went down much easier since I knew what to expect, but my stomach still burned in protest at the offensive liquid I'd dumped in it.

After my eyes stopped watering, I noticed I was being cheered on by the group for my perseverance and smiled. What was the big deal?

"Holy crap, Millie! You're a champ!" Chucky yelled. "Do you drink a lot? You just about finished that thing off!"

Maggie, already tipsy, took another sip and handed the flask back to a teetering Lenny. "No, she doesn't-ever. Neither do I." She said with a smile.

"Noop. Sure don't. That stuff tastes like crap, though."

"I agree," Maggie said. "But I think you just took more than I've had the whole time we've been here in those two swigs. You feel anything?"

I stopped for a minute and thought about it. I could feel a warmth spreading over me, but I wasn't sure that had anything to do with it because I'd never been drunk.

I sure did feel a lot more relaxed, though.

"I feel warm, but that's about it. Plus, I spit most of that first one out."

"Okay. Well, don't drink anymore. Somebody has to drive us home."

"Not a problem. I'd rather drink garbage juice than that stuff."

As the night went on, we all just sat around and chitty chatted about music and other teenagerly pursuits. I had a couple more sips from the flask while Maggie wasn't looking, but aside from that cozy warmth and the fact that I was extremely relaxed now, I couldn't tell I'd had anything. I wasn't worried about driving anymore, that's for sure.

It didn't seem like we'd been there long when Chucky checked his watch.

"It's a quarter after 11!" he yelled in a panic. "I was supposed to have you home ten minutes ago!"

Maggie and I scooted off the hood of the car, but as soon as my feet hit the ground the double dose and few extra sips of whiskey I'd had hit me all at once and my heels got tangled in my dress.

I fell down, but didn't much care. As a matter of fact, I thought it was freaking hilarious.

129

"Whoa!" I said watching the world spin. "This is like Merry Go Rounding, only funner."

Lenny had already started the car and was waiting on the rest of us. "Come on! We're late!"

"Oh, you quit being bossy!" I yelled at him while swatting hands out of my face. "I'm only having a good time!" I tried to get up on my own but fell back down again.

"Millie, take my hand, you idiot. We have got to go!"

I reached up to take it like she asked, but my vision had become a wee bit blurry and I missed it the first few times. She grabbed hold of one arm, Chucky got the other and they eventually got me on my feet.

I was teetering, but I was up.

"What is that?" I said pointing down the road. It looked like a swarm of mutated lightening bugs to me at first, but after looking a little harder I realized it was a set of headlights.

I heard Maggie curse, Lenny started banging on his steering wheel and Chucky burst into tears and started crying like a little girl.

"What is so bad?" I asked, clueless.

With a sigh that sounded like a girl resigned to a difficult fate, Maggie said, "It's the police, you lightweight. We're screwed."

Thanks to a hearty dose of adrenaline, I felt a little of my buzz drift away.

Chucky decided at that moment to have a full on panic attack and between his dramatic crying and pacing, he was driving me nuts. "We cannot get arrested! We can't! We can't! They'll kick me off the golf team, for sure!"

I yanked myself free of Maggie's hold and punched Chucky in the arm as hard as I could. "Knock it off, spaz! We don't care about your stinking golf team!"

Once he'd stopped his wigging out, we all stood there helplessly and watched the car come to a stop and park in front of us.

"We can do this." I whispered to everyone around me. "Just be normal."

The door to the police car opened and, what do you know, it was Officer Unibrow, otherwise known as Officer Wells, from the DMV incident. Did we only have one policeman around here, or what?

With the same swagger and overconfidence he had the last time I'd met him, he strutted over to us and, one by one, looked at us really closely. We were all lined up in front of Lenny's car, so the headlights gave him enough light to see us clearly.

"Miss Crantz, you and I seem to be destined to meet each other quite often. You ever get that driver's license?"

While I didn't realize it at that very moment, my attempt to hide the slight slur in my speech was a complete failure. I tried so hard to conceal it, I just ended up over enunciating everything I said and made it worse.

"Yes, sir it does. My friends and I were just up here checking the place out and talking."

I was having trouble thinking and it took me a minute to remember what his other question was.

"And I did get my license, but I had to wait a couple of months because Mr. Spinner was in a coma and they wouldn't allow me to retake it until they had his results. I was real glad he didn't die."

"Me too. Me too. Well, this is private property and you kids know you aren't supposed to be up here, right?"

"No, sir. No siree, Bob! I thought this was like a nature reserve or something."

A nature reserve? No siree, bob? What in the hell kind of response is that?

I am a moron.

I glanced to the other members of my group and hoped one of them would chime in with something suave. Not one of them so much as looked at me. The wimps.

Not unsurprisingly, he didn't respond to my stupid answer and instead walked up to me and started to sniff. He got so close to me that I was afraid to breathe.

Once he was finished with me, he did the same thing to everyone else before walking back to his car.

He said something into his radio and emerged with a small black box and a bag full of clear plastic straws.

As he pulled a new straw from the bag and attached it to the little black box, he asked all of us our names and wrote them down as we spoke them on a thick plastic clipboard.

Is it just me, or do a lot of people carry clipboards around these days?

"Have any of you been drinking tonight?" He asked smugly.

The no's that came from our group were unanimous.

What? Like we were going to tell a policeman that we were drunk and under aged. No thank you.

He walked up to me first and held out the little black box. "Miss Crantz, I'm going to need you to blow into this little straw until I tell you to stop."

I was in no kind of position to argue, so I did what he asked. Once I was finished he walked back and wrote it down on the clipboard of doom and went on to repeat that process with everyone else.

I knew things were bad when another policeman arrived. The two officers had a small conversation and finally made their way back to our lineup of hooligans to deliver their verdict.

"Your breathalyzer tests all read above the legal limit for intoxication in Kentucky, so myself and Officer Douglas here are going to place you under arrest for Public Intoxication. We'll take you down to the jail and get a hold of your parents. Does anyone not understand this?"

Chucky started his crying all over again, but the rest of us just nodded silently because we knew there was no way out of this one. We'd been caught red handed.

One by one, we were handcuffed, read our rights (like in the movies) and put in the cruisers. Maggie and I went in one and Lenny and Chucky went in the other.

While neither one of us spoke to the other, we were both scared out of our wits. We'd just been arrested-like, for real arrested even.

I wasn't so much scared to go to jail as I was terrified to have to face my parents when they found out what happened.

I am so screwed.

20 JAILHOUSE CONFESSIONS

Jail is not a nice place to be. It smells like sweat, body odor, metal and desperation.

The guards look at you like you're an idiot and the other prisoners look at you like they might want to eat you and wash you down with a tall glass of homemade prison hooch.

Being booked into jail is a lot like you see it on TV. You get fingerprinted, your mug shot is taken and somebody frisks you from your head to your toes. Fortunately, my underage status kept me from having to bend over, if you know what I'm saying, so I happily thanked God for that small blessing.

After answering a few questions about myself and going through the entire routine, I was handcuffed to a metal chair in the booking room to wait on a guard to come and take me to my cell.

My cell. I was going into a cell. A real one.

My insides had already been turned into a nervous mush, but just thinking about who I might have to share a room with absolutely terrified me. It took everything I had not to break down in tears, but I'd managed to stave them off this long, so I figured why start now?

A tall, abnormally muscular female guard came in and unlocked the cuff that was holding me to my chair. I rubbed my wrist and stood up.

"You're Millicent Crantz, correct? Booked for Public Intox?"

"I am," I replied defeated. "That's me."

For a lady as muscular and tough looking as she appeared to be, her face was full of sympathy as she looked at me in my pitiful state. "It's okay, honey." She said softly. "I don't think much will happen. I don't know your parents, but I would say they're who you need to worry about."

I couldn't say much to that because she was right. My mom and dad were going to crap their ever loving pants when they found out.

"Before I take you to your cell, we're going to let you have your phone call. The judge sent an order that you're to contact your parents and explain the situation yourself."

That news went down like bad medicine and my stomach did a huge flip flop. Then, without so much as a warning, I threw up.

Luckily, it only hit the tips of the guard's shoes before she bounced away from me. She went over to a phone on the wall and called for a janitor.

My guard came back over and, after carefully skirting the puke in the floor, put her hand on my shoulder to comfort me. "It'll be okay, let's just call them up and get it over with."

She handed me a wet napkin to clean myself off with and allowed me a few minutes to collect myself.

"I am so sorry." I said looking at her.

"It's okay, honey. You aren't the first person to ever throw up on me. We have people in here that throw their poop on you just because you're livin'. A little puke isn't any big deal."

"Thank you. This day has sucked."

She smiled and we walked over to a desk where she handed me a clunky phone receiver. I numbly rattled off my phone number, she dialed it and quicker than I would have liked, it started to ring.

My mom answered on the first ring and I knew she'd been in a panic over my not being on time for curfew. Instead of stringing her along with excuses, I got right to the point.

"I've been arrested" I said. Even I could hear the quiver in my voice. I rested my forehead against the cold brick wall and waited for the onslaught of screams and curses on the other end of the line.

"Millie, you've come up with some seriously good stories, but this one takes the cake. Okay, I'll play along. What do you mean, arrested?"

"Mom, I mean arrested. Thrown in the clink. Doin' time. Making nice with a large woman named

Bertha who protects me from inner-prison gangs in return for a pack of Lucky Strikes and a late night cuddle."

Aside from some heavy breathing, all I got in return was absolute silence. My mom was about to lose it. I have to come clean before she commences with the yelling or else I'll never get her to hear me out.

Besides, what would my future cellmates think of me if I cowered down to my mommy?

I took a deep breath and prepared myself to confess. I'm a convict now, I told myself. Convict Millie is tough as nails. Convict Millie don't take no crap off nobody.

"It wasn't my fault!" I yelled through the sudden rush of tears and panic.

So much for super tough Convict Millie. Convict Millie is a pansy.

I was alternating between tears of desperation and pure horror while I explained what happened. My mom was using words that I'd never heard come out of her mouth before. More than once she started yelling so loud I had to hold the phone away from my ear to protect my eardrum.

The female guard was still standing nearby and I knew she was hearing our entire conversation. I was being dressed down by my mom and she knew it.

After she'd finished screaming at me, she said she and my dad would come down to get me and slammed the phone down so hard the noise echoed off the walls of the room I was standing in.

I handed the receiver back to the guard and felt about as defeated as I could possibly get. "That went well," I said sarcastically.

She just nodded her head in sympathy and took me by the arm. I guess this is the part where I get to go to the actual cell. Great.

She led me down a long corridor that was extremely bright. It had so many florescent lights in the ceiling you had to squint just to be able to see where you were going. The walls and the floor were painted a light blue and made the walk seem like you were ascending into heaven on a bright blue cloud , even though you knew you were about to enter the gates of hell.

We reached a door and I heard a loud buzz. The door popped open and we walked through it and right into the mouth of the lion's den.

The cells went on forever and I was shocked to see that a lot of people were asleep even though every light in the place was on.

Unfortunately, there were a few women still wide awake and they'd noticed my entrance. It was obvious I was scared to death and they could tell I was young, so that made me a target for a lot of really lovely hoots, hollers, whistles and a few comments that made my toes curl. My dress was not helping matters, either.

"Hey, now! Lookie here! We got the prom queen coming down the Blue Mile!"

"What up, little momma! You gonna be popular in here!"

Thankfully, my guard shut them up before it could get any worse.

"Here we are," my guard said. "Number three!" she yelled into a video camera mounted in the ceiling. Two seconds later I heard another buzz and the cell door slid open.

"In you go," She said, guiding me in by the arm. "We'll come and get you when your parents get here, but until then you're going to have to stay here. And, don't worry. You won't be put with any of the other women since you're underage."

Well, some of that was a relief. I think.

I walked over and sat down on my cot. The cell itself was sparse and the bed, if you can call it that, was basically a slab of concrete with a couple of itchy looking blankets thrown on top.

I looked at the toilet and noticed that there wasn't any kind of partition or privacy curtain to hide behind if you needed to use it. The stainless steel it was made of looked like it might not be the warmest seat in the house, either. Basically, if you needed to do your business you would be have to deal with a frozen ass and an audience.

I decided to hold it-like forever.

The mirror above the sink was made of the same kind of steel as the toilet and kind of reminded me of a circus mirror. I walked over and checked it out, unsurprised to see that it made my head look like it was shaped like a light bulb.

The floor was a drab, grey concrete and for a reason I don't think I want to know, there was a big drain in the middle of it that smelled funny.

"Nice place." I said to nobody in particular. My words echoed off the walls and I jumped a little.

"Yeah, it's a real high class place, jail. What did you expect, little girl? This ain't the Ritz. You find chocolates on your pillow in here, it ain't actually chocolates, if you know what I'm sayin'"

I walked over to the bars of my cell and looked up and down the hallways to see if it came from a guard, but there wasn't anyone there.

I also gave my pillow a glance to see if I'd received any chocolates and was happy to find that I hadn't.

Whoever it was spoke again and I realized it was coming from my next door neighbor. "What did they get you for?" She asked.

"Public Intoxication," I replied tentatively. "What is your name? I'm Millie."

There was a pause before she answered, as if she was trying to decide if she wanted to answer that question or not. "Treva, but my friends call me the Big NB. And before you ask why I'm here, I'll tell you. I hurt somebody real bad, and that is all you need to know."

I couldn't see her, but I could hear her as clearly as if she was standing right next to me. I shuddered a little bit at her last sentence and tried to think of something to say back, but didn't have much else to add to that.

Plus, she hurt somebody real bad. I didn't want to tick her off, ya know?

"Don't be afraid of me, Millie. I was in a real bad place when it happened and I don't just run around doing bad things for fun like those sickos you read about in the news. Some of them mofo's is some sick dudes."

"Okay," I said, following her lead. "I got not even all the way drunk with some friends while I was supposed to be at a dance. Then, I got arrested. My mom and dad are on their way here now to bail me out and then kill me."

Her laughter carried over to my side of the concrete wall between us and I smiled. For a woman whose life was in such disarray, her laugh still had a hopeful ring to it. "Oh, girl. You in a mess, for sure. Them parents of yours, they beat you?"

I was a little taken aback by her bluntness and the question itself was so foreign to me that I had to think for a minute before I answered. "No way! They're good people. They're just extremely mad at me right now, which is understandable considering I broke both rules and laws this evening."

"Good for you, honey," she said. "Ain't everybody got parents like that so you're a lucky one. My daddy beat the hell out of my momma and I for years until I decided I'd had enough of that man and put a stop to it myself. It ain't no kind of way to live, I'll tell you that for sure. When he wasn't beatin' us, he was bein' one of them sick dudes on the news I was talkin' 'bout."

The matter of fact way in which she spoke was punctuated with an obvious sadness. It broke my heart to hear that anyone would ever have to go through something so terrible. My dad would never mistreat my mom or my family and I was able to live my life inside of a bubble where things were safe and the bad stuff only happened in movies. She was living proof that there was fact in all of that terrible fiction.

"I'm so sorry," I said sincerely.

"Ain't no need for you to be sorry for my lot in life. It is what it is. My momma's safe now and I can be glad of that and I use it as my comfort in here when I get to thinking on things too much. You ought to be sorry for putting your parents through this kind of crap, though. They be good to you, you be good to them-simple as that. Take it from somebody who knows-love and family ain't meant to be taken for granted."

"You're right. You are so right." I couldn't say anything more than that because she'd already said it all.

"Okay, then. Imma' get some sleep now. I'm being transferred up to Riverside Women's Correctional Facility tomorrow to serve out my sentence. 30 to life with a bunch of crack heads and crazies is a long time, but I ain't worried. Imma' big girl and can take down some crack heads, you better believe that."

"Wow," I said seriously. "You certainly have a good attitude about it. I'm scared to death just being in here."

"Girl, it's all good in the hood. Life is what you make it and all that. Like I said, I got my comforts and that's all I need."

I didn't reply, but only because I was so shocked that anybody could have a positive outlook on the possibility of life in prison.

"Alright then, I'm out. These jails think waking you up at the ass crack of dawn is a good time. You go home and take your punishment like a woman and move on past it."

I had several more questions, like what it was she did to that bastard dad of hers, but I kept it light. She may have been nice, but I still didn't want to make her mad. "Can I ask you one more question before you go to sleep?"

"Sure. Go 'head."

"What does the NB in Big NB stand for?"

"'Big N' Badass, cause that is what I am!"

I laughed for the first time since I'd seen police lights earlier and it felt good. She made me solemnly swear I would honor her advice and take my punishment like a woman, and our conversation came to an end.

I decided a rest might be nice and eyeballed my cot. Maybe I'll get lucky and wake up tomorrow morning in my own bed, I thought to myself. Maybe it's just a bad dream?

Yeah, right.

After everything I'd been through thus far, I was exhausted. I gave in and decided I'd rest for a few minutes, so I laid down on my concrete bed. The covers had apparently been shipped in directly from the sandpaper plant and I was worried I might chafe my face off if I moved around too much. I looked at the pillow for a few seconds it before shoving it off into the floor. I was still a little weirded out over the whole pillow chocolates thing.

I must have dozed off because the sound of my cell door slamming open and the deep voice of my guard yelling at me scared the bejeesus out of me. I jumped so high I ended up rolling into the floor.

"Crantz! You're free to go! Quit lollygagging in the floor. Your parents are waiting."

"What?" I asked groggily. I rolled over and found that my nose was two inches away from the drain in the floor. This close the smell was stronger and I gagged a little bit. I don't know what they put in there, but I'm guessing it would be something along the lines of bodily fluids and detached fingers.

That woke me up and I scrambled off the floor as quick as I could in my heels. I stood up and wobbled around a little bit and my head started throbbing in pain in unison with the beat of my heart. I had to swallow a few times to make sure I wasn't going to throw up again.

My guard decided I might be a little touched in the head so she repeated herself, only this time she said it slowly as if she was talking to a two year old. "You- can- go. Your-parents-are-here. They-are-waiting."

I've never been so happy, or so scared, in my entire life. I was no longer facing the possibility of being shanked or making license plates, and that was a good thing.

I was, however, facing death. My cell neighbor may have killed somebody (or seriously maimed them), but you make George and Earnestine Crantz mad, you may as well kiss your ass goodbye.

I steadied myself as best I could, tried to brush the smell of whiskey, puke and jail off of my now ruined dress, and stood up straight. I'd acted like a horse's ass and I knew it.

After having heard Treva's story, I had no intention of going back on my word to her. What kind of person would I be if I spit in the face of all the good I had in my life?

Sure, most of my friends and family are nuts. But, I love them, and they love me. It's as simple as that.

As I walked outside to face the music, I absent mindedly wondered what happened to my co-arrestees? I'd lost Maggie after we'd been booked, but hadn't seen the boys since they pulled away in the police car. Whatever it was, I'm sure it was nothing good.

My guard opened a big heavy metal door that led out to a waiting room of sorts, and there they all stood. They were my judge, my jury and my executioners-otherwise known as mom and dad.

I was surprised when I saw my Grandma Lucille pop out from behind them still wearing the housecoat and slippers she'd put on to go to bed. She, of course, hadn't forgotten her purse.

"Millicent May Crantz, you are a dingbat!" she said, sounding madder than I'd ever heard her. "If I wasn't afraid I'd break my own wrinkly ass trying, I'd come over there and kick yours." She looked over to my parents and a cruel smile played across her lips. "I don't think I'm going to need to bother, though. You have a date with your parents."

Damn.

21 CRIME AND PUNISHMENT

The ride home was miserable because not a soul in the car, even Grandma Lucille, spoke to me. You know things are bad when my grandma is quiet.

My body was stiff from my nap on all that concrete, but my head was worse. Every time I turned my head too fast, or breathed, it would throb in protest.

We finally got back home and I have never been happier to see our house. All of the lights had been left on and the soft light escaping from the windows made it look comfortable and homey.

I got out of the car and everyone followed. I'd just walked through the door and did my best to run to my room, but my mom wasn't having it.

"Exactly where do you think you're going?" she spit at me.

I turned around and looked at her for the first time since they'd picked me up. Her face was pinched in anger and worry.

My dad and grandma were standing behind her, both of them with their arms crossed across their chests and both of them were equally as angry as my mom. I felt like I was standing in front of a firing squad just waiting on someone to pull the trigger and put me out of my misery.

"To my room?" I said in a whisper.

My dad looked at me incredulously. "Not a chance. Living room, now."

I hung my head and walked into our family living room and sat down on the couch. As I waited on everyone else to come in, I took my shoes off with a sigh.

My mom and dad both came in and sat down on the loveseat and Grandma Lucille went off to bed. I guess she'd said her piece at the police station.

My mom was tapping her foot and my dad was leaned forward looking at his clasped hands. My mom was the first to speak.

"What in the hell were you thinking? Tell me. I am dying to know why *my daughter* thinks it's okay to go running around in the country with a couple of idiot boys and get drunk!"

I was going to answer her, but my dad beat me to it. "I'll tell you what she was thinking, Earnestine. NOTHING!"

He got up and started pacing around the living room. I felt my palms start to sweat. I had no defense and I knew it, but I still had to wage an internal war with my teenager side not to bite back at them with something hateful.

"I was wrong and I am sorry."

My dad stopped his pacing and my mom just looked at me in shock. You'd think I just told them the end of the world was coming.

"Can you say that again?" my mom asked. She sounded much calmer.

"I said I was wrong and I'm sorry. I honestly don't know what I was thinking."

Again, they just stared at me. I think they'd been waiting on an argument from me, but I wasn't going to even try it on this one. Not only was I busted, but I'd learned a valuable lesson during my conversation with Treva. I had it good and I'd taken that for granted this evening.

"I can't believe it." My dad said. "No denials or screams about how unfair and awful we are?"

"No." I said seriously. "None."

I'd confused my mom so bad she started to stutter and she wasn't making any sense. I did my best to make them understand why.

"Look, I know I screwed up. I knew I was screwing up even when I was doing the screwing up, but I still did it and I honestly couldn't tell you why. The thing is, I met a lady today that hasn't had a really good life and that led to her practically living the rest of her life in a jail cell-which by the way is gross. I guess I just realized that I do have it pretty good, and that is mostly because you two are good people who love me. So, I'm sorry."

My mom started to cry and I felt even worse. "I thought you'd gotten hurt or were dead! I called hospitals, Maggie's parents!" With every word she said, her sobs got louder.

My dad reached down and rubbed her shoulders to comfort her. Nobody said anything for a long time.

Drying her eyes with a tissue my dad had retrieved for her earlier, they got down to the business of punishing me. "You're grounded. And I mean grounded. I'm not even going to give you a time period for how long-it'll just be until I don't want to strangle you anymore."

I nodded my head.

My dad finally chimed in with his ideas. "And you are going to Uncle Earl's for an hour every day after school to clean. I was over there the other day and noticed he'd started collecting curtain rods, so you can help him organize those. He's also got a large pile of pickle jars in an upstairs bedroom, some of which still have pickles in them. You can clean those up as well."

"Can't I clean here?" I begged. "Uncle Earl's house smells like burnt hair!"

"No!" my mom yelled back at me. "You will go to Earl's."

I moaned in protest, but got no sympathy from either one of them. Their stony stares were enough to shut me up.

I was grounded for an undefined period of time and I had to go to Uncle Earl's house-and clean.

Jail sounded really nice right now.

They dismissed me to my room and I went as fast as my blistered feet would carry me. After a quick shower I practically dove into bed. Before I put my head on it, however, I did catch myself checking my pillow out.

Hey, you never know.

My cotton sheets and padded mattress were glorious compared to the concrete and sandpaper beds they had in the clinker. I wiggled around and reveled in the comfort of it before I finally relaxed.

Laying in the dark, I thought about Treva. She was probably still sleeping in that uncomfortable bed, waiting to be woken up by a cranky guard who would load her on a bus with barred windows and whisk her away to a place that was probably much, much worse than the one she was in now.

I wondered what she'd actually done to her father that landed her there in the first place. I got the feeling that it went way beyond a simple beating. After years of abuse, her anger must have been off the scales and when she finally decided to fight back she couldn't stop herself.

I can't say I blame her much. I could say that there is no way I would ever hurt my own dad, but if he was a bad man? Who's to say for sure what somebody would do in that situation unless they've actually been there?

I do hope she finds some kind of peace of mind one day. After a life that hard, she is certainly entitled to it.

While Treva may be a stranger to me, she taught me that no matter how much I may feel like my life is difficult or unfair, it could always be worse.

Much worse.

One thing I can say with certainty--I'll never forget her.

22 DEEP THOUGHTS

I'd been sitting at the base of the same angel statue for well over two hours and my butt had gone completely numb. Actually, it started going numb about an hour ago, but I was too tired to bother with it. Now I'm not even sure if I still have one at all.

Slowly, and very much like a granny, I stood up. I did a little dance around the front of the statue to unstiffen myself and rubbed my hind end in the hopes that it would regain some its lost blood flow.

I needed to walk it off, so I went back the way I'd come towards the grave I started out at in the beginning. Maybe my Fairy Rudemother would pop out of the sky and tell me I was done with all of this business and let me go home.

A girl can dream.

My clothes were finally dry, but my red wool sweater was covered in streaks of dried mud and my skirt was absolutely ruined.

I reached up to my hair to check the damage and wished I hadn't. The first thing my hand touched was a giant dirt clod that had hardened into a rock. I'd have to pull out hair to get it out, so I didn't even bother. I would imagine all of the dead folk hanging out around here don't mind if you hair is a little messy.

My shoes on the other hand looked as spotless as they were when they were given to me earlier. I don't know how I managed to keep them clean with all the mud I've rolled around in, but sure enough-they still look brand new.

Score one for Millie.

As I walked up the little roadway that ran through the middle of the cemetery, I thought about Treva. Actually, I've thought about her many times in my life. I never saw her face or found out what she'd done to her dad, or even the extent of what he'd done to her and her mom, but none of that ever really mattered to me. What did matter was that a stranger had taken a minute to give up just a little piece of what she'd learned in her life-and she did it without an ounce of bitterness.

I still wonder what happened to her. I actually tried looking her up once and never found her. It was like she'd vanished into thin air.

I did keep my promise to her and did the time in penance for my crime.

I spent almost a month going over to my Uncle Earl's house after school on the days I didn't have to work. Most of my time there consisted of me sorting through random piles of stuff he'd collected over time.

On my last day, I was tasked with cleaning out a hallway closet and a Slinky fell on my head and tangled itself up in my hair. My mom spent two hours trying to get it out before we had to go to the professionals. I ended up looking like a psychotic Mary Lou Retton by the time the beautician was done with me.

But, I did eventually get released out on parole. Needless to say, I never visited Happy Mountain again.

Maggie had been banned from going out of her house after school and spent her time grounded helping her mom out with housework and doing a lot of reading. Her mom and dad had come and gotten her like mine had, but her parents made her sit in jail until morning instead of getting her as soon as she'd called like mine did.

Poor Maggie.

Lenny was the one who got into the most hot water. He still had the flask on him when they frisked him. He actually ended up having to go to court and got sentenced to community service for a while.

Chucky didn't get much at all in terms of punishment. I hoped he'd at least gotten grounded. As far as I was concerned, his parents needed to get that kid some serious therapy.

What a weirdo.

It goes without saying that Chucky and I were no soul mates. To be quite honest, just the thought of ending up married to a guy like that gives me the willies.

I do hope he finds somebody that is willing to put up with his crap, but I feel sorry for whoever she is.

I managed to keep as far away from Chucky Peabody as I possibly could after the whole dance debacle. Unfortunately, I did have an encounter with girlfriend of his who happened to be someone I was about as fond of as I was Chucky.

23 FOUR LEGGED THREATS

Winnie Hinkleman has been a thorn in my side and a pain in my behind since third grade when she stole my Trapper Keeper with the picture of a unicorn on the front. She swore she didn't, but our teacher found it in her desk and she ended up getting a paddling for it.

We've hated each other ever since.

So, here we are, one week before our high school graduation having a pissing contest in the middle of the hallway at school.

She'd accused me of flirting with her boyfriend. Regardless of the fact that I had a boyfriend of my own and haven't spoken to the guy she was dating in over a year, she just wouldn't hear of it. I was a liar, a flirt and a floozy.

My boyfriend of the moment, Matt Moody, whom I'd been dating for a record three months now, was standing beside me laughing while Winnie did her whole head bobbing and hollering thing.

"Matt, I heard she did it and I believe it. Chucky wouldn't lie to me like that. He's honest and loving and," Looking at me pointedly she hatefully added, "*Loyal!* Unlike some people I know."

I rolled my eyes. As if I would flirt with Chucky Peabody? I saw the guy almost pee his pants the night we all got arrested. That isn't a quality I find attractive in a man.

Still talking, and getting louder by the second, she was now calling attention to our argument and people were starting to gather around.

"Okay," I said, holding my hand up. "You need to be quiet. You're like a gnat or something. I've been trying to swat you away since third grade with no luck and I'm tired of looking at you."

She looked at me as if I'd said I wanted to tie her to the back of my car and drag her through the city.

I thought about that for a second and smiled. That isn't too bad an idea really.

"Are you…are you *threatening* me?"

"Are you….are you *kidding me*?" I spit back, mocking her.

"I bet you wouldn't be so smart if I shoved a four legged table up your ass sideways, would you?"

That stopped me for a minute while I tried to process what she'd said. I don't believe I've ever heard a stranger threat in my entire life.

"Well, I don't guess I anybody would feel very smart if someone physically assaulted them with furniture."

With that she threw her hands up in the air, flipped me the bird and walked away.

"See ya!" I hollered down the hallway.

"Wow," Matt said. "She's something, huh? If she did that thing with the table I'd always have somewhere to sit my drinks and do my homework, I guess."

I laughed at that and gave him a hug. My short frame and his 6'4 stature didn't mesh very well. I sometimes felt like I was trying to climb the side of a building just to get a hug in.

But he sure was cute. Aside from being tall he had jet black short, curly hair, a dark complexion and a pair of bright green eyes that I found so attractive it almost made my teeth sweat.

I was gazing at him lovingly when I heard Maggie coming up behind me yelling. "Crantz! You and Winnie, huh?"

"Geeze," I said, pulling away from Matt. "News travels fast."

"Yeah, I just talked to Gemma Blake and she told me that Winnie told you she was going to shove a loveseat up your butt."

"Actually, it was just a four legged table, so it could be for any room of the house. And, she was going to shove it in there sideways."

Maggie started laughing and cocked her eyebrows at me. "You know, you don't have anything to worry about with Winnie. She's a pretty big girl, but you're all short and spry, so I bet you could outrun her. Besides, she'd get about halfway to you before those Baywatch boobs of hers beat her unconscious."

"Oh, geeze!" I yelled. "What is the matter with you? You are so odd."

"Whatever," she said as she popped a piece of chewing gum in her mouth. "You know it's true. Those things are the size of my head."

"You do have a big ol' head." I said laughing.

"Shut it. We need to go or we're going to be late. You ready?"

I was, so I said goodbye to Matt and we walked out to Maggie's car. We'd made plans to go shopping after school for graduation outfits.

"You know," Maggie said suspiciously. "We should have a last big hoorah before we graduate and toilet paper Winnie's house or something."

I started to protest, but she stopped me before I even got started.

"No, wait!" she said, stopping at her car door. "We could do the flaming dog poop gag and watch her get a bunch of flaming poo all over her!"

The idea intrigued me, even though I knew it was a horrible idea. When she and I tried doing things like this, it always backfired and landed us in jail or worse.

"I don't know," I said cautiously. "How are we going to find some poop to put in a bag? And who is touching it? I'm not messing around in dog poop."

She thought for a minute and I saw the light bulb above her head light up. "Squinky!"

Squinky was her dog. She was a mix of poodle and some other unknown breed and was so ugly she was cute. I'd been with Maggie several times when she'd taken her outside to use the bathroom, so I knew Squinks was good for it.

"Isn't that just a little bit gross? We're supposed to be torturing someone else, not ourselves."

"Oh, c'mon, Mil! One last thing before we're out of school. It'll be awesome!"

Once again, my decision making skills failed me and I agreed.

24 PRANKING THE ENEMY

.

We canned our shopping trip and spent over an hour that afternoon following Maggie's dog around her backyard.

According to Maggie, who claimed to have seen some TV show about this particular prank, all we had to do was set it on fire, leave it on the windshield of her car and run. We would then be rewarded by watching a panicked Winnie pat the flames out with her hands, only to get poop all over them.

I thought it was genius until it all went wrong.

We'd left my house at around 10 at night, which was when we figured everyone was pretty much asleep, or at least in bed.

Winnie lived on one of the main roads through town across from the city park. It was a small, two story house with white siding and yellow shutters that, lucky for us, didn't have a garage. They parked out on the street, so we had easy access to her car.

We were crouched behind a park bench across the street from Winnie's, arguing over who was going to be the one who placed the offensive item on the car and set it on fire.

"Are you sure we're supposed to set it on fire? Now that I'm thinking about it, who puts out fire with their bare hands?"

"I swear to you, this is exactly how they did it on the show. It was great."

After a little more arguing, and a few more protests that we might be doing it wrong, Maggie finally gave in.

We looked like a couple of idiots. Maggie had on a pair of black sweats, a black t-shirt and a pair of black penny loafers, sans socks. She was so pale that the part of her legs peeking out the bottom of her pants looked like glow sticks.

As for me, I was decked out in my finest spy wear-black boots, black tank top and black jeans. I looked like a backup dancer for Paula Abdul.

After mustering up the courage, Maggie sprinted out from behind our hiding place and ran across the street. I couldn't see her really well because the street lights weren't working around the house, but as soon as she set the bag on fire, I knew she'd succeeded. Seconds later, she appeared out of what seemed like nowhere and dove back behind the bench with me.

"Nothing is happening," I said, peeking through the wooden slats of our hide out. "I see flames, but I don't see any lights on."

I was getting impatient. This had been extremely difficult to pull off and I was going to be super mad if it didn't work.

"Give it a rest, already! It will happen, I swear to you it will happen."

Just as I started to spit out a sarcastic reply, a crackling sound caught my attention.

"What's that noise? Is that the car or was that you?"

"Um, maybe it was the car. Should we go look?" She lifted up and peeked over the top of the bench.

"What do you see?" I asked impatiently.

"Nothing, it's still burning."

"You sure you put it in the right place?"

"Yeah, I think so. You run over and look since I already went once."

Taking my turn, I jogged over to take a look at the car. Just as I looked up at the house a light came on in the upstairs window. I hadn't gotten close enough to see what was happening with the bag, but didn't care.

"Millie move! They're coming!"

I ran and jumped behind a garbage can that set a little ways down from the bench with Maggie on my heels. It smelled like rotten eggs and dead things, but at least we were hidden.

"You know, now that I think of it, maybe it was the doorstep you put the bag on."

I felt my face go white. "What! You said it was the car!"

"That's it! You put it on the doorstep and they step on it to put it out. Then, they get poop on their shoes!"

Fear paralyzed me. The car was now making a lot of noise, smoke rising even faster and the popping noise increasing in volume to the point that there was no doubt we'd screwed up-yet again.

Surly we've set some kind of world record by now.

I looked over at Maggie and watched the reality of the situation wash over her face.

"Damn. My bad."

Just as we were about to make a break for it, a very unattractive man in a pair of tighty whities walked out of the house, groggily rubbing at his face. He hadn't even had time to assess the situation before the car started to sizzle and, finally, burst into a full-fledged fire.

Maggie and I ran like hell. A mile and a half later we heard a very loud explosions followed quickly by sirens. And even though we were a pretty good ways away, I am pretty sure I heard the loud curses of a very angry man.

"This is what happens when you don't do your research." I said to nobody in particular. "Cars explode, people get mad, old men in yucky underwear loose an eyebrow and you spend the next year of your life worrying that the police might find your DNA on a windshield wiper."

When we got back to my house we were sweating, nervous and nauseous. My dad was laid back in his recliner watching the 11 o'clock news.

"Hey, girls. You hear any sirens outside? One of your mom's friends just called and said old Mr. Gussler's car just blew up. He lives up on Flint Avenue next door to that Winnie girl you all go to school with. Apparently he just missed getting blown up himself. It's those damned foreign cars people buy."

Maggie and I just stood there, mouths hanging open and hearts beating wildly.

Not only had we become honest to goodness felons, but we'd blown up the wrong damn car. Thank goodness we were going to graduate soon. At least I'd have my high school diploma before I land myself in prison.

Why must life be so difficult?

25 REVELATIONS

I'd finally made it back graveside and surveyed the mess I'd made earlier. I did my best to reorganize the flowers, but a few of them were in such bad shape they were ruined.

I felt a little guilty about what I'd done, but I was still mad about my situation, so I probably don't feel as guilty as I should.

I know I've been put here for a reason, but I still don't know what reason that is. I've considered the fact that maybe this is my version of the afterlife, or even that I am taking my Get into Heaven test and flunking horribly.

But I don't feel dead. I'm walking, I'm talking and I can feel the cold of the night approaching deep down in my bones.

"You aren't dead, my dear." Said a very familiar voice from behind me.

I whipped around and there she was, smiling at me. "You're back! How exactly do you get here? Do you float in on a cloud or just snap your fingers and transport yourself?"

"Oh, don't be so dumb, Millie. That kind of stuff doesn't actually exist. You've watched entirely too much TV."

She was still smiling at me and I had the sudden urge to knock her down. Her vague and sometimes incomplete answers were getting on my nerves. I wouldn't, of course, but only because my momma taught me better than to go pushing around little old women, no matter how aggravating they may be.

My face must have given away the way I was feeling because she went from smiling to serious all at once.

"What?" I asked. "Why are you looking at me like that?"

"I'm trying to figure out how to tell you something without you getting madder than you already are."

Uh oh. Why did that sound not so great to me? Maybe I was about to get zapped into hell for not passing my This is Your Life quiz.

"Okay, then." I said slowly. "What kind of bad are we looking at here? Is it hellfire and brimstone bad or is it just a small kind of bad-like when you get a splinter?"

She shook her head at me in disbelief and smirked. "You are the strangest girl I believe I have ever known."

Just to see if I could trip her up and get some extra info, I slipped in a, "So, how long have we known each other."

She just cocked an eyebrow and gave me a sarcastic smile. "Don't be weird, Millie. You know I can't tell you that."

I tried again. "And, exactly who do you take your orders from?"

She didn't say a word and I just kept on going. Maybe I could irritate her to death and get her to tell me just so I'd leave her alone.

"Is it God? Have I been kidnapped by Jigsaw and this is a test? Am I going to have to cut somebody's eyeball out to find a key to escape?"

I was still talking when a surprisingly loud *shut up!* rang through the entire cemetery. I almost pee'd my pants for real that time. She sure had a good set of lungs for such an old lady.

I did as she asked and just stood there with my hands on my hips staring at her. I didn't know what else to do.

After looking at me like she was contemplating my death, she finally exhaled and relaxed a little. Her face said we were getting ready to get down to some serious and somewhat unpleasant business, and I felt my heart start to jump around in my chest.

"Come with me, Millie. And please, do not talk. If you talk, I will be forced to kick you're whiney little rear end and I don't really want to have to do that."

I nodded and followed her quietly.

We were heading back towards the angel statue down the road and I wanted to tell her that I'd already been there, but thought better of possibly making her mad and ruining any chance I had of making it back into the real world.

As we walked, she was stoically quiet. I looked at her face a little closer hoping to gauge what she was feeling at that moment, but it wasn't giving anything away.

I hate to be corny considering our surroundings, but her silence scared me to death.

She stopped in the road and turned to face the angel statue. I took a couple of steps towards it, assuming that was where we were headed, but she grabbed the sleeve of my sweater to stop me.

Her face was lined with worry and grief, making her look much older than she already was. She didn't move, but for five minutes solid she didn't take her eyes off of that angel.

Then, as if she'd gotten some kind of an answer to an unspoken question, she righted herself and started back down the road.

I quickly realized we were walking to the gates that led outside and felt my heart leap a little at the thought of walking through them and getting out of here.

The cemetery walls were tall and made out of a dismal grey stone that looked to be extremely old and weathered. The only way to get in and out was through the large iron gates in front of us, and they rose much higher than even the wall itself.

The steel was curled in a decorative fashion and the top part held the name. The lettering was a bold, freshly painted white that stood out in stark contrast to the black steel behind it.

Riddle Cemetery.

"You've got to be kidding me? All these years I haven't bothered to see what this place was called, and its *Riddle Cemetery*." I couldn't help but chuckle a little at the irony.

During the day, the gates were left open for people to come and go as they pleased. It only occurred to me just now that I hadn't even thought to check if they were open earlier. I had taken this woman at her word and not even considered the fact that she might a big old fibber.

"Well?" I said, throwing my hands out to my sides. "What is this big thing you need to tell me?"

She took a deep breath and finally, started to talk. "Have you wondered why you haven't left here on your own? Just walked over here yourself and gone right on home?"

"As a matter of fact," I said sincerely. "I was just thinking about that just a minute ago. The answer is no. I just took you at your word and, to be quite honest, I don't know why."

"I want you to go over and try to open them."
She pointed at the lock on the gate and I looked back
at her like she was crazy.

"I can see the padlock on it and they're locked.
Why bother?"

"Just try."

I didn't see any reason to argue with that, so I
walked over and grabbed a hold of the padlock. As I
lifted it up, I noticed that it had been put through the
chains, but whoever had done it hadn't actually locked
the padlock. I slipped it off, unwrapped the heavy
chain that held the gates together and pushed hard.

And, wouldn't you know it, they opened right up.

"What the hell?" I said, now more than just a little
mad that I'd been so stupid. "You mean I've been
running around in here like this all this time and I
could have just walked right on out?"

She just nodded her head. That infuriated me
even more, so I started to yell.

"This is wrong. This is all wrong. I need you to
tell me what in the hell is going on right now, or so
help me God I am going to lose it!"

She looked positively defeated. I was expecting
some kind of a rebuttal, but she didn't hit me with
anything but a whole lot of silence.

"Can't you even *speak* to me now? I deserve an
answer!"

"I can't give you answers, you little twit. I've told you that a thousand times already and you don't seem to be getting it through that thick head of yours!"

I stopped for a minute and took a few deep breaths to try and calm myself down. I wasn't as mad at the woman standing in front of me as I was myself for being such a moron.

Nothing, and I mean nothing, made sense.

"Do you want to leave?" she asked.

"Hell yes I want to leave! Duh!"

"No, I want you to really think about that. I want you to take a minute and remember this day from start to finish and tell me what you remember. Tell me what you felt when I first handed you those shoes. Tell me why you got mad and ripped those flowers to bits?"

I thought about it for a few minutes before I answered her. "Honestly, I don't remember if I traveled here in a plane, a train or an automobile. I remember thinking I was late because I was the last one to arrive. I know that when I walked up to join the crowd, my heart was breaking and I knew without a shadow of a doubt that whoever was inside of that coffin was important to me in a way that I can't explain."

I took a deep breath and continued.

"When I first saw you I knew you felt the same way I did about them. Your face was so grief stricken that I could swear I felt it from where I was standing. And when you gave me these shoes, I believed you when you told me that I was here for a reason. It feels strange to say it out loud, but not for one minute did I ever question what you'd said to me. I didn't like it, I was confused and I still am, but even looking at you right now I still feel like that. There is something inside of me that knows I am where I am supposed to be right now and that; somehow, my being here is my fault."

"The question is, Millie Crantz, are you going to walk out of those gates and leave, or are you going to stay and figure this out?"

I looked up at the tall iron gates and sighed. "I don't know."

She walked over towards me, put her hands delicately on each side of my face and looked me straight in the eye, "I want you, just for a minute, to step away from the gates and really examine this cemetery. Then, I want you to tell me what you see."

I did as she asked and started to look around at my surroundings.

At first all I could see was what everyone else sees when they're here-headstones of various shapes and sizes, flower arrangements and the weathered remnants of the old and forgotten flowers scattered about here and there, as well as a few sparse stone benches that had been placed around in different areas.

And, of course, there was the angel, ever mindful of her place here and always on duty. She is the only comfort to be found in a word full of loss and sadness.

My eyes began to trace the outline of the stone wall that surrounded us and I was surprised to see how far and wide it actually ran. It seemed to go on forever and it was a good reminder of how big this place was.

That's when it hit me.

"It's me, right?" I asked with tears now running slowly down my face. "This cemetery is me. I built the wall to keep the people out, but I haven't locked the gates just yet."

"That's right." She said, putting a hand on my shoulder. "But that isn't all."

"Am I dead?" I asked her, my tears now coming a little quicker. "Have I died?"

She looked at me and cocked her head to the side with a smile. "No, you're still breathing, aren't you? You're crying and you can feel, right?"

"Yeah, but how on earth did I end up trapped inside of my own metaphor? And what about the funeral? Whose was it?"

"That is something you're going to have to figure out for yourself. It's true that the somebody in that grave is important to you, but once you really start to thinking about it, you'll remember who."

I felt my shoulders slump. I'd had this ginormous epiphany about myself, yet I still didn't feel any closer to figuring any of this out.

"How, exactly, am I supposed to do that?"

"Millie, when people come here to visit a loved one, they bring with them the memories of the time that those loved ones were living--the good, the bad and the ugly. They're more meaningful than any picture or memento left behind. They are a big part of who they've become and in some cases, what they aspire to be."

Life, the hustle and the bustle and the drive to succeed in the world, had taken me away from those memories, and I now knew what she meant. I was floating, aimlessly, and I'd lost my footing along the line and forgotten who I am.

"But where did I go wrong?"

Smiling sarcastically, she looked at me like I was an idiot. "Why do you ask questions that you know good and well are going to get a cryptic answer?"

"I'm hoping you're senile and will eventually let an answer slip out on accident."

"Not going to happen. I'm sharp as a tack and I know you entirely too well to fall for any of your crap."

I wiped the tears from my face and chuckled.

"Now, then. You need to dry those tears up and get to figuring out where you've gotten off course. I have to go and I won't be back for a while."

"Wait!" I yelled, grabbing her sleeve to make sure she didn't mysteriously poof out of here before I asked her one last question. "Where do I start?"

"Are you serious? Where you left off, of course. It's in there," she said quietly while pointing at the area where my heart is. "You're just going to have to work to find it."

I let go of her sleeve and sighed. That is a lot of living to get through and I'd be here forever if that was the case.

"No, Millie. Just go with what pops in your head first. There is a reason certain memories stand out and those are the ones you'll need to dig through."

I was tired, but I'd found new resolve in this latest newsflash. I could do this, I thought to myself. It was my life, after all.

"Oh!" she added. "One more thing."

She ambled over to the gate and pulled the padlock off. "You'll need to lock this."

"I have to lock myself in?" I asked in disbelief.

"The decision to stay or go, by the way, is permanent. You're either doing this, or you aren't. Now which is it?"

I paused for a second and considered that. I'd have been more comfortable knowing I could leave at any time and just forget this ever happened, but I guess it would at least take away the temptation to completely give up.

"Fine." I bit out. I walked over, took the padlock out of her hand, pulled the gates together and after pulling the chains tightly around the middle, shut the lock with a click.

The noise it made when it locked echoed all over the cemetery and I felt a chill run down my spine at the finality of it.

Before I turned back around to face my uncertainties, I knew my Fairy Rudemother was gone, and I was alone again.

It was now just me, the dead, our memories and the possibility of an eternity spent here wallowing in them.

Dear Lord, please help me navigate my way out of this one. Spending the rest of my forever in this place did not sound like a good time.

With that, I straightened my skirt, squared my shoulders and walked back over to the angel. Even though I know she's nothing but a pretty rock, being near her is comforting.

26 BISCUIT AND THE DRAGON NOODLE

With high school graduation only a day away, I was on the lookout for a new job for the summer. The dancing doughnut gig was a real killer in the hotter seasons and I wanted some air conditioning.

I'd seen an ad in the paper for a waitressing job at a place called The Dragon Noodle in Ashford, a town over from Flatwoods. I'd never been to the place and don't remember ever seeing it, but it was just a ten minute drive from my house so I decided to give it a try.

It took me a few tries to finally locate it because it was small and tucked away in a part of Ashford that I'd never been in. It sat facing a back alley and the entrance looked a little old, but it didn't look unsafe.

The sign out front was a big light up dragon with The Dragon Noodle written on the front in giant red letters.

"Must be a Chinese place." I said as I parked my car in the parking lot that sat across from it.

Walking in, my eyes had a little trouble adjusting to the dark atmosphere. The dining room floor was blocked off by a big wall, so I walked over to a small cashier's desk where an Asian man wearing a pink suit, blue tie and a pink and blue fedora was leaned against the counter looking bored.

When he saw me, he stood up and smiled. His hair was a bright blue and just barely peeked out from underneath his hat. The pink and blue was an interesting combo.

"Welcome to the Dragon Noodle, can I help you?"

His voice was extremely high for such a tall man and it caught me off guard for just a minute. I just stood there looking at him like an idiot.

"Ma'am," he said slowly. "Can I help you?"

I snapped out of it. "Yes, yes, sorry. I'm here about the ad in the paper for the waitressing job."

"Excellent!" he said, eyeballing me a little closer now. He stretched out his hand and I gave it a shake back. "My name is Wang, but my friends call me Biscuit."

"Biscuit? Why?"

"I don't really know, it just kind of happened that way. Anyways, I'm the manager here, so let's go on back to my office and grab you an application. Do you have any, um, waitressing experience?"

"No, sorry. But I'm a good worker." I replied, hoping I sounded confident.

"That's okay, you gotta start somewhere, right? Follow me."

I nodded my head and fell in step behind him. As we walked, I could hear a loud techno music coming from somewhere and wondered what kind of place was next door.

"Where is the actual restaurant part?" I asked confused as to why we'd not seen it.

He pointed over to a set of blacked out double doors to our right just as we passed it. "Right through there. We like our customers to have privacy while they're here, so we keep it kind of blocked off to those who come and go."

"Okie dokie." I replied, thinking it was strange. I had no idea that people considered privacy an important part of the dining experience.

We hit another door at the end of a long hallway and Biscuit took a set of keys out of his pocket to open it. He swung open the door and went in, but I paused at the doorway, shocked by the room's décor.

The walls were covered in blue and pink fuzz and the ceiling had been covered in mirrors. His desk was a normal desk, but the chair was a giant throne looking seat with a high back and had been reupholstered with more of the blue and pink fuzz.

No wonder he kept it locked.

He dug around in his desk and pulled out an application while I looked at myself in the ceiling. He had to literally wave the paper in my face before I realized he'd found it.

"Just fill this out and bring it back when you can. We'll set up an interview then."

"Nice office," I said, not meaning it. "I like the fuzz. It's...interesting."

"You like that? I get a good deal on it from a guy I know who works at the carpet store up on Frame Street."

I made a mental note to never buy carpet at Frame Street.

We walked back down the hallways and just as we got to the two darkened double doors that led to the dining area, Biscuit stopped and turned to look at me. "You want to see the place?"

"Sure!" I said, wondering if it was also big and fuzzy.

He opened the doors and the techno music I'd heard before made my eardrums vibrate it was so loud. It hadn't been coming from some other place; it was coming from inside that room. There was a thick padding on the door and I realized they were soundproof.

Biscuit gallantly gestured for me to go first and I did, very cautiously. As soon as my foot crossed the threshold, I gasped.

The floor was set up like any other restaurant and so was the bar, but there was a stage up front set with various sized poles and lots of neon lights. There were four extremely nude women sliding around those poles and the men sitting along the stage were holding up cash in the hopes that one of them would come and get it.

If that wasn't enough, I also realized that the waitresses didn't have any shirts on.

I turned and ran so fast I'd forgotten the door was pull, not push, and ran face first into it, smashing my nose. It immediately started to burn and I felt the warmth of a small trickle of blood hit my top lip as I scrambled up off of the floor.

I grabbed the door handles while listening to Biscuit's muffled yells about where I was going and I was out of there like a shot. I didn't quit running until I got to my car.

I locked the doors and took a quick look at my nose before wiping it off with my shirt sleeve. I wasn't worried about ruining it because they'd touched the floor inside when I fell, so I'd be burning them anyways.

I can't even leave a room with dramatic indignation without making an ass of myself.

After all of this, the dancing doughnut job sounded like a dream come true.

27 MILLIE CRANTZ GROWS UP

We'd finally made it to graduation day. And Amen to that.

Unfortunately, my accident at the Dragon Noodle had left me with two black eyes from the nose to door impact. I did my best to cover it in makeup, but it didn't do me any good.

The girl's in our class were all wearing white caps and gowns and the boy's outfits were maroon. As I looked around the student union at all the faces I'd known after years in school together, I couldn't help but feel a little sentimental.

That sentimentality, however, was getting old fast. My mom, grandma and Verna had taken so many pictures of me I was starting to feel like I had my own paparazzi.

'Okay!" I said, putting my hands in front of my face to block more snaps. "I think you have enough."

I'd posed with everyone in the family (both together and one by one), Maggie, Chris, some random girl I didn't know and even our principal.

"Oh, Millie. Quit! You only graduate once!" My mom squealed. Geeze Louise, the woman is relentless.

My dad was being my dad, just standing around doing his best to stay away from all the women, but still managing to look at me with pride. I smiled back at him and he gave me a quick wink.

Maggie and Chris came over just as the lady coordinating our ceremony told everyone to line up in their places, so we didn't get to talk. The three of us were bummed that we didn't get to sit together, but our names didn't allow it since everyone was put in alphabetical order.

I saw Matt walking by holding the hand of a juinior girl whose name I didn't know. We'd broken up because I'd heard they'd been sneaking out of study hall to make out.

Looks like that rumor was true. I gave them both a dirty look and went back to the task at hand.

My walking partner was a weird little guy named Landon Crazzner. I didn't know him very well, but he'd been in my Kindergarten class so I recognized him.

As we stood together waiting on the processional to start, I looked over at him. He was short, had dark hair that looked like it had been hit with a hard dose of static electricity and I could tell he was wearing jeans under his graduation gown.

"Hey," I said, tugging on his gown sleeve. "You remember that time in Kindergarten when we made homemade butter in a jar? You were afraid of the cornbread we ate with it for some reason and started crying. That was so funny."

He just looked at me, clearly not impressed at my attempt at small talk. Of course, reminding a teenage guy that he'd once been afraid of cornbread is a bad way to start a conversation.

"Sorry," I said. "I'm nervous."

He nodded his head, still looking disgusted, and I didn't attempt any more conversation after that.

Mercy of mercies, the graduation song started to drift out to our ears from the gym and the line started to move.

As we walked in, we were greeted with cheers and people screaming the names of the kids they'd come here to see graduate. I looked up to a spot I thought I'd heard mine and saw my family standing up clapping and screaming until they were red in the face.

Heck, Wally had even deemed this day special enough for his toupee.

My Aunt Verna was blowing me kisses and my mom was standing next to her waving and drying her eyes with a tissue. Above them on the bleachers sat my very bored looking brother and my dad who, even though I couldn't tell for sure from this distance, looked a little teary eyed himself.

My Grandma Lucille, however, was screaming *I love yous* at the top of her lungs and clapping wildly as if she was at a rock concert. She went to blow me a kiss, but I guess her finger got caught on her teeth and pulled them out. As she flung her arm out to throw the kiss at me, her teeth went flying and landed somewhere down in the bleachers below them.

I found myself, for once, not embarrassed, but laughing so hard I barely found my seat.

I sat down and looked back up at them. My Aunt Verna had apparently retrieved grandma's teeth for her because Grandma Lucille had them wrapped up in the bottom of her silk shirt wiping them off. With a smile, she popped them back in and gave me a thumbs up.

I do love my family.

The speeches were long and boring, and more than once I caught Landon dozing off. As a courtesy, I'd give him the occasional elbow nudge to wake up him.

The names of all my classmates were called one by one and I caught even myself getting a little teary eyed at the hugeness of the milestone. This was it.

No more Millie the Kid. I was an adult now.

I heard various roars of delight coming out of the Crantz section in the audience as I walked up to get my diploma. I shook the hands of the school's administrators and went back to my seat. I watched thoughtfully as the rest of my friends became adults as well.

The ceremony finally came to a close and we all tossed our caps into the air in declaration of our achievements and walked outside to wait on everyone else.

Maggie found me first and Chris was soon to follow. We all hugged, rehashed our graduation experience and before long, the rest of my family found me.

The hugs I got from each of them were long and hard and you could tell they were sad I was growing up.

I was, though, and found myself looking forward to what came next in my life. College was on the list, but I hadn't made any decisions about where just yet. I planned on figuring that out this summer while I danced my ass of in the giant doughnut from hell.

Everyone had gone over to congratulate Maggie and her parents and I looked at all of them with a smile. I was lucky to have them, all of them, even when they were being strange.

If that makes me strange, well then so be it. What can I say?

I'm a Crantz.

ABOUT THE AUTHOR

Mandi Hayes-Spencer was born and raised in Flatwoods, Kentucky. She is the wife of 34 year old loveable hippie-type and the mother of an 11 year old boy wonder.

She is a columnist for The Greenup County Beacon and has been published in various print and online publications. She also sometimes blogs for Grey Television's mom focused website at Momseveryday.com.

When not writing, she enjoys working her day job as a cook in an elementary school cafeteria. While there, she spends time cooking, serving well balanced meals to the kids, singing random 80's songs at the top of her lungs, crafting oranges into fruit art and, much to the dismay of her coworkers, making extremely big messes.

She currently resides in Kentucky with her husband, son, three cats and a very spoiled schnauzer, Stella Blue.

Learn more about Mandi and her upcoming releases on her website:

www.mandidoeslife.com
www.facebook.com/mandihayesspencer